序　言

「中級英語檢定測驗」每一個高中生都要參加，不參加等於沒有高中畢業。將來沒有通過「中級英語檢定測驗」，就無法申請好的大學。未來的趨勢是，高中三年的教科書，只能當輔助閱讀資料，所有的高中生，都要積極準備此項檢定考試。

「中級英語檢定測驗」初試部份，分為聽力測驗及閱讀能力測驗。其中，閱讀能力測驗包含詞彙與結構15題、段落填空（即克漏字）10題、閱讀理解（即閱讀測驗）15題。本書專門訓練同學的閱讀能力。

「中級英語檢定測驗」中的閱讀測驗，與「**大學入學學科能力測驗**」及「**指定科目考試**」的英文閱讀測驗相同。為了出題客觀，我們請多位老師命題，蒐集不同的資料，經過1383位同學實際測驗後，證明使用這本書，必可提升閱讀能力。

本書每篇文章都有翻譯，每個句子都有文法分析，較難單字都有註解，節省讀者查字典的時間。學習出版公司的目標就是，每一本書，都要有詳詳細細的解說，不避重就輕。有看不懂的地方，是編者的責任。

歡迎讀者來信，或打電話給我們。有了你們的批評，我們才會更進步。這本書另附有「學生用書」，提供給高中老師教學之用。

編者　謹識

本書製作過程

　　本書 Test 7 與 Test 8 由李麗莎老師命題，Test 11 至 Test 13 及 Test 21、23、26 由廖曄嵐老師命題，Test 16、19 及 Test 24 由唐慧莊老師命題，Test 1 至 Test 6，Test 9、10、14、15、18、20、22、25，及 Test 27 至 Test 50 由謝靜芳老師負責。命題後，詳解由謝靜芳老師執筆。全書完成後，先由命題老師校對完，又請 Andy Swarzman、Laura E. Stewart、Bill Allen 三位外籍老師詳細校對。全部測驗題均經過劉毅英文家教班同學實際測驗過，同學的閱讀能力有顯著的提升。

本書另附有學生用書，售價 120 元。

再版的話

　　這一本閱讀測驗，經過 1383 位優秀的高二和高三同學，實際測驗過。我們以此試題，舉行「**全國高中英文閱讀測驗大賽**」，參加的同學包含：建中、北一女、師大附中、成功、中山、景美、延平、松山等學校同學。

　　同學在測驗之初，約在前 10 回，覺得做起來很吃力，答題速度又慢，但是，到了 10 幾回以後，很多同學就豁然開朗，答題速度加快，感覺到做起來輕鬆。連續做到 30 回以後，考過 2 小時之後，就開始覺得體力不支，頭昏眼花。一般同學拼命地寫，在 150 分鐘內，大約只能做到 40 回，只有少數幾位同學，能夠完全做完 50 回。

　　經過這次研究，我們覺得，本教材非常適合高一、高二、高三的學生使用。

　　高一：每 10 分鐘考 1 回，考後老師立刻講解。
　　高二：每 15 分鐘考 2 回，考後老師立刻講解。
　　高三：每 30 分鐘考 5 回，考後可讓同學自行看自修本。

　　只有在班上考試的時候，才有氣氛，使同學專心接受閱讀測驗的訓練。如果自己在家研讀，需要有很大的毅力。

劉　毅

TEST 1

Read the following passage, and choose the best answer for each question.

The girls arrived at the airport on time, but William did not. His plane was late and it was nearly one o'clock by the time he had taken care of all his business at the airport. Both he and the girls were quite hungry by that time, so they decided to eat lunch in the airport restaurant before they started home. Besides, they had a lot of things to talk about. William wanted to hear the latest news of his family and friends, and Helen and Betty wanted to ask questions about his work overseas. Helen was also interested in her brother's plans for the year ahead.

1. Which of the following statements is true?
   (A) William went to the airport to meet his sisters who had returned from abroad.
   (B) The plane was right on schedule.
   (C) They had lunch before they left the airport for home.
   (D) Helen was so hungry that she didn't care about William's future plans.

2. Which of the following statements is NOT true?
   (A) The plane didn't arrive until one o'clock in the afternoon.
   (B) The girls arrived at the airport earlier than William did.
   (C) William had been away from home for some time.
   (D) William had all his business settled at the airport before he ate lunch with Helen and Betty.

3. What do we know about William's work?

   (A) He works in the airport.
   (B) He is in business.
   (C) He works in a foreign country.
   (D) He works on a ship.

4. When did the girls arrive at the airport?

   (A) They arrived before William did.
   (B) They arrived at one o'clock.
   (C) They arrived after lunch.
   (D) They arrived late.

5. Why was William late?

   (A) He missed his flight.
   (B) There is a large time difference between his hometown and where he works.
   (C) The airport was crowded.
   (D) The flight was delayed.

TEST 1 詳解

The girls arrived *at the airport on time*, ***but*** William did not.

His plane was late ***and*** it was *nearly* one o'clock *by the time he had taken care of all his business at the airport*. Both he and the girls were *quite* hungry *by that time*, ***so*** they decided to eat lunch *in the airport restaurant **before** they started home*.

女孩們準時到達了機場，但是威廉卻沒有，因為他的飛機誤點。而當他把入境手續都辦好時，時間都已經快一點了。那時他和女孩們肚子都很餓，所以他們決定在動身回家前，先在機場餐廳吃午餐。

take care of 處理　　business ('bɪznɪs) *n.* 事情
start (stɑrt) *v.* 出發；動身

Besides, they had a lot of things to talk about. William wanted to hear the latest news *of his family and friends*, ***and*** Helen and Betty wanted to ask questions *about his work overseas*. Helen was *also* interested in her brother's plans *for the year ahead*.

此外，他們也有很多事情要談。威廉想知道他家人和朋友的近況，而海倫和貝蒂則想問問他在國外的工作情形。海倫也對她哥哥來年的計畫很感興趣。

latest ('letɪst) *adj.* 最新的；最近的
overseas ('ovɚ'siz) *adj.* 在國外的
ahead (ə'hɛd) *adj.* 在將來

1.(**C**) 下列敘述何者為眞？

    (A) 威廉去機場接從國外回來的姊妹。

    (B) 飛機很準時。

    (C) <u>他們在從機場回家前已吃過午餐。</u>

    (D) 海倫很餓，所以並不關心威廉對未來的計畫。

    * meet (mit) *v.* 接   abroad (ə'brɔd) *adv.* 在國外
    leave…for~ 離開…前往~   *care about* 關心；在乎
    on schedule 按照時間表

2.(**A**) 下列敘述何者為非？

    (A) <u>飛機直到下午一點才到達。</u>

    (B) 女孩們比威廉早到機場。

    (C) 威廉離開家已有一段時間了。

    (D) 威廉在和海倫以及貝蒂吃午餐之前，就把機場的手續都辦好了。

    * settle ('sɛtḷ) *v.* 處理

3.(**C**) 關於威廉的工作，我們知道什麼？

    (A) 他在機場工作。   (B) 他經商。

    (C) <u>他在外國工作。</u>   (D) 他在船上工作。

    * *in business* 經商；做生意

4.(**A**) 女孩們何時到達機場？

    (A) <u>她們比威廉早到。</u>   (B) 她們一點鐘到。

    (C) 她們吃過午餐才到。   (D) 她們遲到。

5.(**D**) 威廉為什麼遲到？

    (A) 他錯過了班機。

    (B) 他的家鄉和工作的地方有很大的時差。

    (C) 機場很擁擠。   (D) <u>班機延誤。</u>

    * flight (flaɪt) *n.* 班機
    time difference 時差   delay (dɪ'le) *v.* 延誤

TEST 2

Read the following passage, and choose the best answer for each question.

In order to qualify for a single room in a university dormitory, you must be a full-time student who has completed the necessary number of hours to be ranked as an upperclassman. Applicants for such university housing are required to submit completed applications to the Office of Student Housing at the beginning of the semester they are requesting such housing. Students will be notified regarding the status of their application by the sixth week of class. Private dorm rooms will be assigned to qualified students on a first-come, first-served basis.

1. According to this reading, in order for a student to get a single dormitory room he must _____
   (A) be rich.
   (B) be married.
   (C) be a junior or senior.
   (D) have superior grades.

2. When should a student apply for a single dormitory room?
   (A) Before the semester begins.
   (B) At the beginning of the semester.
   (C) A few weeks after the semester begins.
   (D) At the end of the preceding semester.

3. What is the main topic of this reading?

   (A) Applying for a Dormitory Scholarship
   (B) Applying to Share a Dormitory Room
   (C) Regulations for University Admissions
   (D) Regulations for Applying for a Private Dormitory Room

4. Why are the rooms assigned on a first-come, first-served basis?

   (A) There are a limited number of single dormitory rooms available.
   (B) There are enough dormitory rooms for all students.
   (C) There are more single dormitory rooms than students who want them.
   (D) There are not enough students who want single dormitory rooms.

5. Students will be informed of the status of their application _____

   (A) at the end of the semester.
   (B) one month before the semester ends.
   (C) in the middle of the semester.
   (D) one and a half months after the semester begins.

TEST 2 詳解

In order to qualify for a single room in a university dormitory, you must be a full-time student *who has completed the necessary number of hours to be ranked as an upperclassman.*

想要能有資格擁有一間單人的大學宿舍，你必須是個全日制的，以及修完必修學分的高年級生。

> *qualify for~* 有資格~　　single〔'sɪŋgḷ〕*adj.* 單人的
> dormitory〔'dɔrmə͵torɪ〕*n.* 宿舍 (= *dorm*)
> full-time〔'fʊl'taɪm〕*adj.* 全日制的　　*be ranked as~* 被列為~
> upperclassman〔͵ʌpɚ'klæsmən〕*n.* 高年級學生；大三、大四學生

Applicants for such university housing are required to submit completed applications *to the Office of Student Housing at the beginning of the semester they are requesting such housing.*

申請這類大學宿舍的人，在學期初，就要繳交填好的表格至學生住宿處。

> applicant〔'æpləkənt〕*n.* 申請人　　housing〔'haʊzɪŋ〕*n.* 住宅
> submit〔səb'mɪt〕*v.* 提出；交出　　complete〔kəm'plit〕*v.* 填寫 (表格)
> application〔͵æplə'keʃən〕*n.* 申請表　　request〔rɪ'kwɛst〕*v.* 要求

Students will be notified *regarding the status of their application by the sixth week of class.* Private dorm rooms will be assigned to qualified students *on a first-come, first-served basis.*

到了上課的第六週，學生就會知道申請的情況。私人宿舍將以「先到者先供應」的原則，分配給有資格申請的同學。

notify（'notə,faɪ）*v.* 通知　　regarding（rɪ'gɑrdɪŋ）*prep.* 關於
status（'stetəs）*n.* 情形　　assign（ə'saɪn）*v.* 分配

1.（**C**）根據本文，若想擁有一間單人宿舍，必須是

(A) 有錢的。　　　　　　　　(B) 已婚的。
(C) 大學三年級或四年級。　　(D) 成績優良的。

* junior（'dʒunjə）*n.* 大三學生　　senior（'sinjə）*n.* 大四學生
superior（sə'pɪrɪə）*adj.* 較優秀的　　grade（gred）*n.* 成績

2.（**B**）學生應該何時申請單人宿舍？

(A) 學期開始前。　　　　　　(B) 學期初。
(C) 學期開始後幾個禮拜。　　(D) 上學期末。

* preceding（prɪ'sidɪŋ）*adj.* 之前的

3.（**D**）本文的主題是什麼？

(A) 申請宿舍獎學金　　　　　(B) 申請合住宿舍
(C) 申請大學入學之規定　　　(D) 申請私人宿舍之規定

4.（**A**）房間為何以「先到者先供應」的原則來分配？

(A) 空著的單人宿舍有限。
(B) 宿舍房間足夠所有的學生使用。
(C) 單人宿舍的數量比申請的學生多。
(D) 想要單人宿舍的學生不夠多。

5.（**D**）學生何時會收到申請結果的通知？

(A) 學期末。　　　　　　　　(B) 學期結束前一個月。
(C) 學期中。　　　　　　　　(D) 學期開始後一個半月。

TEST 3

Read the following passage, and choose the best answer for each question.

The six year old is about the best example that can be found of that type of inquisitiveness that causes irritated adults to exclaim, "Curiosity killed the cat." To him, the world is a fascinating place to be explored thoroughly, and it is constantly expanding through new experiences, which bring many eager questions from members of any group of first graders, as each one tries to figure out his place within the family, the school, and the community. There are adults who find it quite annoying to be presented with such inquisitiveness. But this is no purposeless prying, no idle curiosity! It is that quality, characteristic of the successful adult, inherent in the good citizen — intellectual curiosity.

1. According to this passage, inquisitiveness is _____
   (A) an annoying quality.
   (B) only found in the six year olds.
   (C) killing the cat.
   (D) characteristic of the successful adult.

2. The author's attitude in this passage toward children is one of _____
   (A) despair.
   (B) confidence.
   (C) sharp criticism.
   (D) indifference.

3. "Curiosity killed the cat" as used in this passage probably means to suggest that an inquisitive person is likely to _____

   (A) succeed.
   (B) suffer injury or harm.
   (C) raise many eager questions.
   (D) become a good citizen.

4. A word that could meaningfully replace "prying" as used in this passage is _____

   (A) exploring.   (B) expanding.
   (C) support.   (D) fascination.

5. In writing this passage, the author's purpose is _____

   (A) to defend the inquisitiveness of the child.
   (B) to criticize such inquisitiveness.
   (C) to discuss the pros and cons of curiosity.
   (D) to report the result of a study on curiosity.

TEST 3 詳解

The six year old is about the best example *that can be*

found of that type of inquisitiveness that causes irritated adults to

exclaim, "Curiosity killed the cat."

六歲這個年紀的人，大概是我們所能發現的最好例子，是那種會令生氣的
大人們大喊：「好奇心害死了貓（過於好奇會惹上麻煩）」最典型的例子。

* old 在此當名詞用，作「～歲的人」解，six year 是名詞做形容詞，來表示
單位，故用單數形（詳見文法寶典 p.87）。of that type…cat. 是第一個 that
子句中的主詞補語。再看下例：

We can find it of use.⇨ It can be found *of use*.
主詞補語

inquisitiveness (ɪn'kwɪzətɪvnɪs) *n.* 好奇；好問
irritate ('ɪrə,tet) *v.* 激怒　　irritated ('ɪrə,tetɪd) *adj.* 生氣的
exclaim (ɪk'sklem) *v.* 呼喊
curiosity (,kjurɪ'ɑsətɪ) *n.* 好奇心

To him, the world is a fascinating place *to be explored thoroughly*,

and it is *constantly* expanding *through new experiences*, *which*

bring many eager questions from members of any group of first

graders, *as each one tries to figure out his place within the family*,

the school, and the community.

對他而言，這世界是個可徹底探索的迷人地方，而且透過新的經驗，這個世界正不斷地擴展中。這些經驗帶來了很多任何一年級學生，都渴望得知答案的問題，因爲他們都試著想去理解，自己在家庭、學校和社會中的地位。

* and 連接 To him，…thoroughly 和 it (= *the world*) is…community 兩個對等子句。其中 which bring…community 是補述用法的形容詞子句，補充說明 experiences，而 as 則引導副詞子句，修飾 bring，表原因。

　　fascinating (ˈfæsn̩ˌetɪŋ) *adj.* 迷人的
　　explore (ɪkˈsplor) *v.* 探索　　thoroughly (ˈθɝolɪ) *adv.* 徹底地
　　constantly (ˈkɑnstəntlɪ) *adv.* 不斷地
　　expand (ɪkˈspænd) *v.* 擴展
　　eager (ˈigɚ) *adj.* 熱切的；渴望的
　　grader (ˈgredɚ) *n.* ～年級學生　　***figure out*** 理解
　　place (ples) *n.* 地位；身份
　　community (kəˈmjunətɪ) *n.* 社區；社會

There are adults *who find it quite annoying to be presented with*
　　　　　　　　　　　　　形式受詞　　　　　　　　　　　　眞　　　正
such inquisitiveness. ***But*** this is no purposeless prying, no idle
受　　詞
curiosity!

有許多大人會覺得，面對這樣的好奇是相當討厭的。但這絕非無意義的探問，也絕非無聊的好奇！。

* 「be no + (動) 名詞」(做補語用)，其中的 no 是「絕不是」的意思 (詳見文法寶典 p.171)。

　　annoying (əˈnɔɪɪŋ) *adj.* 討厭的；惱人的
　　present (prɪˈzɛnt) *v.* 向～提出
　　purposeless (ˈpɝpəslɪs) *adj.* 無目的的；無意義的
　　pry (praɪ) *v.* 刺探；打聽
　　idle (ˈaɪdl̩) *adj.* 無目的的；無聊的

It is that quality, (***which is***) *characteristic of the successful adult,*

(***which is***) *inherent in the good citizen — intellectual curiosity.*
那是一種特質，成功的成年人的特性，好公民生來就有的 —— 求知慾。

> * characteristic…adult 和 inherent…citizen 是兩個由補述用法的形容詞
> 子句，所簡化而來的形容詞片語，補充說明 that quality。intellectual
> curiosity 則是 that quality…citizen 的同位語。

> quality (ˈkwɑlətɪ) *n.* 特性
> characteristic (ˌkærɪktəˈrɪstɪk) *adj.* 特有的
> ***be characteristic of*** 是～的特性
> inherent (ɪnˈhɪrənt) *adj.* 生來就有的
> citizen (ˈsɪtəzn̩) *n.* 公民　　***intellectual curiosity*** 求知慾

1. (**D**) 根據本文，好奇

　　(A) 是種討厭的特質。　　　　(B) 只在六歲的人身上發現。
　　(C) 會殺死貓。　　　　　　　(D) 是成功的成年人的特性。

> * annoying (əˈnɔɪɪŋ) *adj.* 討厭的

2. (**B**) 在本文中，作者對小孩的態度是

　　(A) 絕望。　　　　　　　　　(B) 信任。
　　(C) 尖銳的批評。　　　　　　(D) 漠不關心。

> * despair (dɪˈspɛr) *n.* 絕望
> sharp (ʃɑrp) *adj.* 尖銳的；嚴厲的
> indifference (ɪnˈdɪfərəns) *n.* 漠不關心

3. (**B**) 本文中的「好奇心害死了貓。」可能是暗示好奇的人，可能會
　　(A) 成功。　　　　　　　　　(B) 受到傷害。
　　(C) 引起許多熱切的問題。　　(D) 成為一位好公民。

> * injury (ˈɪndʒərɪ) *n.* 傷害　　raise (rez) *v.* 引起
> eager (ˈigɚ) *adj.* 熱切的

4. (**A**) 在意義上能代替本文中 "prying" 「探問」的字是

    (A) <u>探索。</u>   (B) 擴展。

    (C) 支持。   (D) 著迷。

    * meaningfully ('minɪŋflɪ) *adv.* 意義上

      replace (rɪ'ples) *v.* 代替

      fascination (ˌfæsn̩'eʃən) *n.* 著迷

5. (**A**) 在寫本文時，作者的目的是

    (A) <u>爲小孩的好奇心辯護。</u>

    (B) 批評這樣的好奇。

    (C) 討論好奇心的利弊。

    (D) 報導研究好奇心的結果。

    * defend (dɪ'fɛnd) *v.* 爲～辯護

      the pros and cons 利弊；正反兩面

      study ('stʌdɪ) *n.* 研究　　on (ɑn) *prep.* 關於

自己做閱讀測驗，做不下去的時候，可和同學比賽，一起做題目，看誰答對的題目多。

TEST 4

Read the following passage, and choose the best answer for each question.

Omar's army had been victorious over the Persian forces. The conquered chieftain was taken prisoner and condemned to death. As a last boon he asked for a cup of wine. It was brought to him. Seeing that he hesitated to raise it to his lips, Omar assured him that neither was the wine poisoned, nor was there anyone there who would kill him while he drank. Omar added that he gave his word as a prince and a soldier that his captive's life was safe until he had drunk the last drop of wine. At these words, the Persian poured the wine upon the ground and demanded that Omar keep his promise. In spite of the angry protests of his followers, Omar kept his word and allowed his prisoner to go free.

1. Omar assured the chieftain that ＿＿＿＿＿＿
   (A) he would be killed if he drank the wine.
   (B) probably no poison had been dissolved in the wine.
   (C) he was safe until he had drunk the last drop of wine.
   (D) he was a prince and a soldier.

2. The chieftain poured the wine upon the ground _____
    (A) after he had asked Omar to keep his promise.
    (B) after he had drunk a little.
    (C) immediately after Omar had given his word.
    (D) immediately after he had hesitated.

3. The chieftain poured the wine because _____
    (A) he wanted to escape.
    (B) he wanted to be given his freedom.
    (C) he wanted to be alone.
    (D) he was afraid of the angry protests of Omar's followers.

4. The conquered chieftain showed _____
    (A) cleverness.   (B) kindness.
    (C) a sense of honor.   (D) bravery.

5. The best title for this selection is _____
    (A) Omar's Victory.
    (B) An Unworthy Chieftain.
    (C) The Wine of Promise.
    (D) Omar's Honor.

TEST 4 詳解

Omar's army had been victorious over the Persian forces. The conquered chieftain was taken prisoner *and* condemned to death. As a last boon he asked for a cup *of wine*. It was brought to him. Seeing *that* he hesitated to raise it to his lips, Omar assured him *that* neither was the wine poisoned, *nor* was there anyone there who would kill him *while he drank*.

奧瑪的軍隊打敗了波斯軍隊，俘虜了戰敗的波斯首領，並判他死刑。波斯首領要求在他死前，最後再賜予他一杯酒。於是他們就給了他一杯酒。奧瑪看到他很猶豫，不敢將酒舉到唇邊，於是就向他保證，這杯酒沒有毒，而且也不會有人趁他喝酒時殺他。

> victorious (vɪk'torɪəs) *adj.* 勝利的　　forces ('forsɪz) *n. pl.* 軍隊
> chieftain ('tʃiftən) *n.* 首領　　*take sb.* *prisoner* 俘虜某人
> *be condemned to death* 被判死刑　　boon (bun) *n.* 恩賜
> hesitate ('hɛzə,tet) *v.* 猶豫　　assure (ə'ʃur) *v.* 保證

Omar added *that* he gave his word as a prince *and* a soldier *that* his captive's life was safe *until* he had drunk the last drop of wine. At these words, the Persian poured the wine *upon the ground and* demanded *that* Omar keep his promise. In spite of the angry protests of his followers, Omar kept his word *and* allowed his prisoner to go free.

奧瑪又說，他以王子及軍人的身份保證，在這位俘虜喝完最後一滴酒之前，其生命都是安全無虞的。聽到這些話，那個波斯人便把酒倒在地上，並要求奧瑪遵守承諾。儘管屬下憤怒地抗議，奧瑪還是信守諾言，允許他的囚犯自由離去。

add〔æd〕*v.* 補充說　　*give one's word* 保證
captive〔'kæptɪv〕*n.* 俘虜　　pour〔por〕*v.* 倒
demand〔dɪ'mænd〕*v.* 要求　　*keep one's promise* 信守諾言
protest〔'protɛst〕*n.* 抗議　　follower〔'faloɚ〕*n.* 屬下；隨從

1. (**C**) 奧瑪向那位首領保證，
   (A) 如果他喝酒就會被殺。
   (B) 可能沒有毒藥溶於酒中。
   (C) 在他喝完最後一滴酒之前都會很安全。
   (D) 他是一位王子也是個軍人。
   * dissolve〔dɪ'zɑlv〕*v.* 溶解

2. (**C**) 那位首領將酒倒在地上，
   (A) 是當他要求奧瑪遵守諾言之後。
   (B) 是在他喝了一些酒之後。
   (C) 是在奧瑪一說完他的保證之後。
   (D) 是在他一猶豫完之後。

3. (**B**) 那位首領將酒倒在地上，是因為
   (A) 他想逃走。　　　　　　(B) 他希望獲得自由。
   (C) 他想自己一個人。　　　(D) 他怕奧瑪的屬下強烈抗議。

4. (**A**) 那位戰敗的首領展現了他的
   (A) 聰明。　　(B) 仁慈。　　(C) 榮譽感。　　(D) 勇敢。

5. (**D**) 本篇選文最好的標題是
   (A) 奧瑪的勝利。　　　　　(B) 一位卑鄙的首領。
   (C) 諾言之酒。　　　　　　(D) 奧瑪的信用。
   * unworthy〔ʌn'wɝðɪ〕*adj.* 不值得的；卑鄙的
   honor〔'ɑnɚ〕*n.* 信用

TEST 5

Refer to the following timetable:

	Timetable		
Train	Lv. Boston	Ar. Midway	Ar. New York
504	5:10 AM Ex. Sun	7:00 AM	10:45 AM
131	7:10 AM Daily	9:00 AM	12:45 PM
62	9:10 AM Ex. Sat. & Sun.	11:00 AM	2:45 PM
797	10:00 AM Ex. Hol.	11:45 AM	......
234	1:15 PM Daily	3:15 PM	5:45 PM
501	3:40 PM Ex. Hol.	5:40 PM	8:15 PM
236	5:20 PM Daily	7:20 PM	9:55 PM

1. How many times a week does the 9:10 AM train arrive
   in New York from Boston?

   (A) 6 times.　　　　　(B) 5 times.
   (C) 7 times.　　　　　(D) 2 times.

2. What is the shortest elapsed time between Boston and
   New York?

   (A) 5 hours, 35 minutes.
   (B) 5 hours, 5 minutes.
   (C) 4 hours, 30 minutes.
   (D) 4 hours, 25 minutes.

3. You have a luncheon date at Midway on Saturday. What time must you leave Boston in order not to be late?

(A) 5:00 AM. (B) 7:10 AM.

(C) 9:10 AM. (D) 10:00 AM.

4. If you need to leave Boston by 1:30 pm, and arrive in New York before 9:00 pm, which train do you need to take?

(A) 501 (B) 62

(C) 234 (D) 797

5. If you need to arrive in New York every day after 1:00 pm, how many different trains can you take?

(A) 1 (B) 3

(C) 2 (D) 4

TEST 5 詳解

參考下列時刻表：

時　刻　表				
火車班次	起　波士頓		迄　中途市	迄　紐約
504	上午　5:10	星期日除外	上午　7:00	上午 10:45
131	上午　7:10	每日	上午　9:00	下午 12:45
62	上午　9:10	星期六、日除外	上午 11:00	下午　2:45
797	上午 10:00	例假日除外	上午 11:45	……
234	下午　1:15	每日	下午　3:15	下午　5:45
501	下午　3:40	例假日除外	下午　5:40	下午　8:15
236	下午　5:20	每日	下午　7:20	下午　9:55

timetable〔'taɪm,tebḷ〕*n.*（火車、公車等的）時刻表
Lv. = Leave 離開　　Ar. = Arrive 抵達
Ex. = Except 除了…之外
AM = ante meridian（拉丁文 = before noon）　上午
PM = post meridian（拉丁文 = after noon）　下午
Sun. = Sunday 星期日　　daily〔'delɪ〕*adv.* 每天
Sat. = Saturday 星期六　　Hol. = Holiday 例假日

1. (**B**) 上午 9 點 10 分由波士頓開往紐約的火車，一週有多少班次？
   (A) 6 班。　　　　　　　　　(B) <u>5 班。</u>
   (C) 7 班。　　　　　　　　　(D) 2 班。

2. (**C**) 波士頓和紐約之間費時最短是多少？
   (A) 5 小時 35 分。　　　　　(B) 5 小時 5 分。
   (C) <u>4 小時 30 分。</u>　　　　　(D) 4 小時 25 分。

   * elapse〔ɪ'læps〕*v.*（時間）過去

3. (**D**) 星期六你在中途市有個午餐約會，爲免遲到，你必須幾點離開波士頓？
　　(A) 上午 5 點。
　　(B) 上午 7 點 10 分。
　　(C) 上午 9 點 10 分。
　　(D) 上午 10 點。

4. (**C**) 如果你必須在下午 1 點 30 分前離開波士頓，而且在下午 9 點以前到達紐約，你必須搭哪一班火車？
　　(A) 501　　　　　　　　(B) 62
　　(C) 234　　　　　　　　(D) 797

5. (**C**) 如果你每天都必須在下午 1 點以後到達紐約，你可以搭乘的火車有幾班？
　　(A) 一班。　　　　　　　(B) 三班。
　　(C) 二班。　　　　　　　(D) 四班。

時間緊迫時，閱讀測驗可先看題目，再看文章。將文章中，與題目有關的內容劃線，複查起來較方便。

TEST 6

Read the following passage, and choose the best answer for each question.

High in the Swiss Alps many years ago there lived a lonely shepherd boy who longed for a friend to share his evenings. One night he saw three wrinkled old men each holding a glass. The first said, "Drink this liquid and you shall be victorious in battle."

The second one said, "Drink this liquid and you shall have countless riches."

The last man said, "I offer you the happiness of music — the horn."

The boy chose the third glass. Next day he came upon a great horn, ten feet in length. When he put his lips to it, a beautiful melody floated across the valley. He had found a friend.

So goes the legend of the horn. Known in the ninth century, the horn was used by herdsmen to call cattle, for the deep tones echoed across the mountainsides. And even today, on a quiet summer evening, its music can be heard floating among the peaks.

1. What is the topic of this reading?

    (A) The Hobbies of Shepherd Boys
    (B) The Legend of the Horn
    (C) The History of the Swiss Alps
    (D) The Dreams of Shepherd Boys

2. What detail about the shepherd boy does this reading tell us?

    (A) He has a lonely job.   (B) His age.
    (C) His name.   (D) His singing ability.

3. Why did the boy choose to drink the glass offered by the last old man?

    (A) The boy liked the old man.
    (B) The boy didn't like the other old men.
    (C) The boy loved music.
    (D) The boy was thirsty.

4. After the shepherd boy found the horn, he discovered it was _____

    (A) stolen from someone else.
    (B) very easy to carry with him.
    (C) impossible to play.
    (D) like having a new friend.

5. Today the horn is heard in the Swiss Alps _____

    (A) in the spring.   (B) in the summer.
    (C) in the autumn.   (D) in the winter.

TEST 6 詳解

High in the Swiss Alps many years ago there lived a lonely
shepherd boy *who longed for a friend to share his evenings.* *One*
night he saw three wrinkled old men, *each holding a glass.*

多年以前，瑞士境內阿爾卑斯山的高山上，住著一個孤單的牧童，他很渴
望能有一個朋友，和他分享山中的傍晚。有天晚上，他看見三位滿臉皺紋的老
人，每個老人手上都拿著一個玻璃杯。

* One night he saw three wrinkled old men, each holding a
  glass. 因兩句之間無 and 連接，而將後句改爲分詞構句。本句相當於
  One night he saw three wrinkled old men, and each of
  them held a glass.

> Swiss〔swɪs〕*adj.* 瑞士的
> Alps〔ælps〕*n.* 阿爾卑斯山
> shepherd〔'ʃɛpəd〕*n.* 牧羊人　　**long for** 渴望
> share〔ʃɛr〕*v.* 分享　　wrinkled〔'rɪŋkl̩d〕*adj.* 有皺紋的
> glass〔glæs〕*n.* 玻璃杯

The first said, "Drink this liquid *and* you shall be victorious
in battle."

第一位老人說：「喝下這個液體，你在戰場上就會獲得勝利。」

> liquid〔'lɪkwɪd〕*n.* 液體
> victorious〔vɪk'torɪəs〕*adj.* 勝利的
> battle〔'bætl̩〕*n.* 戰爭

The second one said, "Drink this liquid and you shall have countless riches."

第二個老人說：「喝了它，你就會有無數的財富。」

　　countless ('kauntlıs) *adj.* 無數的　　riches ('rıtʃız) *n. pl.* 財富

The last man said, "I offer you the happiness of music — the horn."

最後一個說：「我給你音樂的快樂──號角。」

　　offer ('ɔfɚ) *v.* 給予；提供　　horn (hɔrn) *n.* 號角

The boy chose the third glass. *Next day* he came upon a great horn, *ten feet in length.* *When* he put his lips to it, a beautiful melody floated *across the valley.* He had found a friend.

男孩選了第三個杯子。隔天他發現了一個巨大的號角，有十英呎長。當他把號角靠在唇上吹時，整個山谷就飄盪著美麗的旋律。他終於找到朋友了。

　　come upon 偶然遇到　　lips (lıps) *n. pl.* 嘴唇
　　melody ('mɛlədı) *n.* 旋律　　float (flot) *v.* 飄
　　valley ('vælı) *n.* 山谷

So goes the legend *of the horn.* *Known in the ninth century,* the horn was used *by herdsmen to call cattle,* *for* the deep tones echoed across the mountainsides. *And* even today, *on a quiet summer evening,* its music can be heard *floating among the peaks.*

　　這就是號角的傳說。大家都知道，早在西元第九世紀，號角就被牧羊人用來呼叫牛群，因其低沈的音調能在山間迴盪。甚至在今天，在寧靜的夏夜，似乎還能聽到飄揚在山峰間的樂音。

* 本段第二句相當於 The horn was known in the ninth century, ***and*** it was used by herdsmen…，因對等連接詞 and 連接前後相同主詞的子句，故省略前面部分之主詞，形成分詞構句：Known in the ninth century, it…。

go〔go〕*v.*（詞句等）寫著；說
legend〔'lɛdʒənd〕*n.* 傳說
herdsman〔'hɝdzmən〕*n.* 牧羊人
cattle〔'kætl̩〕*n.* 牛群　　deep〔dip〕*adj.* 低沈的
tone〔ton〕*n.* 音調　　echo〔'ɛko〕*v.* 產生迴響
mountainside〔'mauntn̩,saɪd〕*n.* 山腰；山坡
peak〔pik〕*n.* 山峰

1. (**B**) 本文的主題為何？

(A) 牧童的嗜好　　　　　　　(B) <u>號角的傳說</u>
(C) 瑞士阿爾卑斯山的歷史　　(D) 牧童的夢想

2. (**A**) 本文告訴我們什麼與牧童有關的細節？

(A) <u>他的工作很孤單。</u>　　(B) 他的年紀。
(C) 他的名字。　　　　　　　(D) 他的歌唱能力。

* detail〔'ditel〕*n.* 細節

3. (**C**) 為什麼男孩選擇喝下最後那位老人給他的那一杯？

(A) 男孩喜歡那老人。
(B) 男孩不喜歡其他老人。
(C) <u>男孩喜歡音樂。</u>
(D) 男孩口渴。

4.(**D**) 牧童找到了號角之後，他發現號角

  (A) 是從別人那裏偷來的。   (B) 攜帶方便。

  (C) 吹不出聲音。   (D) <u>就像一位新朋友。</u>

  * carry〔ˈkærɪ〕*v.* 攜帶

5.(**B**) 現在在瑞士的阿爾卑斯山中，何時仍能聽到號角聲？

  (A) 春天。   (B) <u>夏天。</u>

  (C) 秋天。   (D) 冬天。

   如果題目中問到，What is the best title for the above passage? 或 What is the main idea of this passage? 之類的問題時，最快的方法是看第一句和最後一句，或每段的第一句，找出相同的關鍵字（key words），即是答案。

TEST 7

Read the following passage, and choose the best answer for each question.

It is against this background of corruption, revolution, hypocrisy, and greed that the Soong legend begins.

Few families since the Borgias have played such a disturbing role in human destiny. For nearly a century they were key players in events that shaped the history of Asia and the world. Members of the Soong clan became household names — Dr. Sun Yat-sen, Madame Chiang Kai-shek, Generalissimo Chiang, Madame Sun. Others served as China's prime ministers, foreign ministers, finance ministers. They amassed some of the greatest fortunes of the age; T.V. Soong may have been the richest man on earth.

1. Without the unstable situation in China, the Soongs would probably _____
   (A) never have played so important a role in China and the world.
   (B) have achieved more success.
   (C) have become more famous for their dynasty.
   (D) have gone anywhere.

2. From the passage, we know that _____
   (A) the Borgias can't have affected history very much.
   (B) the Soong family were not as important and distinguished as the Borgias.
   (C) only a few families have been as outstanding as the Soong family and the Borgias.
   (D) most families can be as remarkable as the Soongs and the Borgias.

3. According to what is mentioned in the passage, which one is not true?
   (A) Members of the Soong clan were either famous or rich.
   (B) Many families can be compared with the Soongs.
   (C) Few families have been so rich and unusual as the Soongs.
   (D) Many members of the Soong family have served high positions.

4. From which phrase can we infer that the writer doesn't think highly of the Soongs?
   (A) the greatest fortunes
   (B) the richest man
   (C) household names
   (D) a disturbing role

5. Maybe we can say _____
   (A) the Soong family played a minor role in Asian history.
   (B) Asia has been prosperous because of the Soongs.
   (C) no corruption, no Soong success.
   (D) without a revolution, there wouldn't be any corruption.

TEST 7 詳解

It is against this background *of corruption, revolution, hypocrisy,*

and greed that the Soong legend begins.

宋家傳奇的崛起，就是靠腐敗、革命、虛僞，和貪婪的背景。

* 強調句型：「It is / was + 強調部份 + that + 其餘部份」（詳見文法寶典 p.115 ）。

    against〔ə'gɛnst〕*prep.* 以～爲背景
    background〔'bæk,graund〕*n.* 背景
    corruption〔kə'rʌpʃən〕*n.* 腐敗；貪污
    revolution〔,rɛvə'luʃən〕*n.* 革命
    hypocrisy〔hɪ'pɑkrəsɪ〕*n.* 僞善；虛僞
    greed〔grid〕*n.* 貪婪   Soong〔soŋ〕*n.*（姓氏）宋
    legend〔'lɛdʒənd〕*n.* 傳奇；傳說

Few families *since the Borgias* have played such a

disturbing role *in human destiny. For nearly a century* they

were key players *in events that shaped the history of Asia and*

the world.

自從 Borgias 家族以來，很少有家族，能在人類命運中，扮演這麼令人煩擾不安的角色。幾乎在將近一個世紀的時間裏，宋家是構成亞洲和世界歷史事件的主要角色。

* since the Borgias 與 in human destiny 爲表時間的副詞片語，修飾動詞 have played. 而 that shaped…world 爲形容詞子句，修飾先行詞 events。

Borgias 為義大利十四至十六世紀具有影響力的家族。

play ~ role 扮演~角色

disturbing〔dɪ'stɝbɪŋ〕*adj.* 令人不安的

destiny〔'dɛstənɪ〕*n.* 命運　　century〔'sɛntʃərɪ〕*n.* 世紀

key〔ki〕*adj.* 主要的　　player〔'pleɚ〕*n.* 演員

shape〔ʃep〕*v.* 形成　　Asia〔'eʃə〕*n.* 亞洲

Members *of the Soong clan* became household names — Dr. Sun

Yat-sen, Madame Chiang Kai-shek, Generalissimo Chiang,

Madame Sun.

宋家的成員變成家喻戶曉的人 —— 孫逸仙、蔣介石夫人、蔣委員長、孫夫人。

　* of the Soong clan 為形容詞片語，修飾前面的名詞 members。

clan〔klæn〕*n.* 家族

household〔'haʊs,hold〕*adj.* 家庭的

household name 家喻戶曉的人

Madame〔'mædəm〕*n.* …夫人

generalissimo〔,dʒɛnərəl'ɪsə,mo〕*n.* 三軍總司令；最高統帥

Others served as China's prime ministers, foreign ministers,

finance ministers. They amassed some *of the greatest fortunes*

of the age; T.V. Soong may have been the richest man *on earth*.

其他人則擔任過中國的行政院長、外交部長、財政部長。他們積蓄了當代的最

大財富；宋子文可能是世界上最富有的人。

serve as 擔任　　minister〔'mɪnɪstɚ〕*n.* 部長

prime minister 行政院長；首相

amass〔ə'mæs〕*v.* 積蓄（財富）

fortune〔'fɔrtʃən〕*n.* 財富

1. (**A**) 沒有中國的不穩定情況，宋家也許

    (A) 永遠不會在中國，以及全世界，扮演這麼重要的角色。

    (B) 會更成功。

    (C) 因他們的王朝而更有名。

    (D) 會有進展。

    * unstable〔ʌn'stebḷ〕*adj.* 不穩定的

       achieve success 成功

       dynasty〔'daɪnəstɪ〕*n.* 王朝　　*go anywhere* 有進展

2. (**C**) 從本文，我們可知

    (A) Borgias 家族對歷史影響不大。

    (B) 宋家不如 Borgias 家族重要顯赫。

    (C) 只有少數幾個家族能像宋家和 Borgias 家族那麼傑出。

    (D) 大部分的家族都能像宋家和 Borgias 家族一樣顯赫。

    * affect〔ə'fɛkt〕*v.* 影響

       distinguished〔dɪ'stɪŋgwɪʃt〕*adj.* 傑出的

       outstanding〔aʊt'stændɪŋ〕*adj.* 傑出的

       remarkable〔rɪ'mɑrkəbḷ〕*adj.* 顯著的

3. (**B**) 根據本文，下列何者為非？

    (A) 宋家成員不是有名就是富有。

    (B) 有許多家族都可以和宋家相提並論。

    (C) 很少有家族和宋家一樣富裕和不凡。

    (D) 宋家有許多人當過高官。

    * compare〔kəm'pɛr〕*v.* 比較　　serve〔sɝv〕*v.* 任（職）

       position〔pə'zɪʃən〕*n.* 職位

4. (**D**) 從哪一個片語，我們可推論，作者並不敬重宋家？

(A) 最大的財富

(B) 最富有的人

(C) 家喻戶曉的人

(D) 令人不安的角色

* phrase〔frez〕*n.* 片語　　infer〔ɪn'fɝ〕*v.* 推論
think highly of 尊敬；重視

5. (**C**) 也許我們可以這麼說，

(A) 宋家在亞洲歷史扮演不重要的角色。

(B) 亞洲因宋家而繁榮。

(C) 沒有腐敗，就不會有宋家的成功。

(D) 沒有革命，就不會有腐敗。

* minor〔'maɪnɚ〕*adj.* 不重要的
prosperous〔'prɑspərəs〕*adj.* 繁榮的

本書另附有「學生用書」，全班同學一起
考試，比較有氣氛，才做得下去，題目才
做得快。

TEST 8

Read the following passage, and choose the best answer for each question.

Constant change is an integral part of the Communist philosophy. For the entire thirty-eight years of Communist rule in China, the Party's policy has swung like a pendulum from left to right and back again without stop. Unless and until a political system rooted in law, rather than personal power, is firmly established in China, the road to the future will always be full of twists and turns. The wanton use of personal power such as Mao wielded during the Cultural Revolution may yet turn back the clock. Factional struggle for power among the new leaders is almost a certainty, though there will be an interval of superficial unity while each man consolidates his position. The Chinese people will continue to stand on the sidelines, allowed to speak only with an affirmative voice.

1. The Communist Party _____
   (A) has tried hard to stop their pendulum work.
   (B) seems to be in full swing.
   (C) is always changing their policy.
   (D) wants to adhere to steady measures.

2. Based on this passage, we see that _____

  (A) the author believes policy should change.
  (B) the author hopes for simple unity.
  (C) the writer approves of the way Mao ruled.
  (D) the writer prefers a political system rooted in law.

3. According to this passage, we can conclude _____

  (A) new leaders should strive for power.
  (B) the road to the future should be steady and predictable.
  (C) the Chinese should only be allowed to speak well of the authorities.
  (D) the Chinese people should not take part in making the policy of the government.

4. "Superficial" is synonymous with _____

  (A) shallow.
  (B) wanton.
  (C) artificial.
  (D) superb.

5. The writer of this passage _____

  (A) wishes each leader to strengthen his position.
  (B) is opposed to faction fighting.
  (C) thinks that Mao had the power and used it in a proper way and wishes that Mao could come back to rule China.
  (D) wants the Chinese people to show their approval of the policy unanimously.

TEST 8 詳解

Constant change is an integral part *of the Communist philosophy.* *For the entire thirty-eight years of Communist rule in China,* the Party's policy has swung *like a pendulum from left to right* **and** *back again without stop.*

經常改變是共產黨哲學中，不可或缺的一部份。在共產黨統治中國的三十八年中，黨的政策一直像鐘擺，不停地從左擺到右，再從右擺到左。

constant (ˈkɑnstənt) *adj.* 不斷的
integral (ˈɪntəgrəl) *adj.* 不可或缺的
Communist (ˈkɑmjuˌnɪst) *adj.* 共產主義的
philosophy (fəˈlɑsəfɪ) *n.* 哲學
party (ˈpɑrtɪ) *n.* 政黨   policy (ˈpɑləsɪ) *n.* 政策
swing (swɪŋ) *v.* 搖擺
pendulum (ˈpɛndʒələm) *n.* 鐘擺

Unless **and** ***until*** *a political system rooted in law, rather than personal power,* *is firmly established in China,* the road *to the future* will *always* be full of twists and turns. The wanton use *of personal power such as Mao wielded during the Cultural Revolution* may *yet* turn back the clock.

除非或是直到一個以法律，而不是個人權力爲基礎的政治制度，能在中國確實地建立，否則未來的道路必定將充滿曲折與變動。個人權力的濫用，像是毛澤東在文革期間所掌握的權力，可能會使時光倒流。

be rooted in 根植於；牢固地建立於～的基礎上
rather than 而不是　　firmly ('fɝmlɪ) *adv.* 堅固地
twist (twɪst) *n.* 彎曲　　turn (tɝn) *n.* 變化
wanton ('wɑntən) *adj.* 不當的；胡亂的
wield (wild) *v.* 掌握（權力）
revolution (ˌrɛvə'luʃən) *n.* 革命
the Cultural Revolution 文化大革命
turn back the clock 使時光倒流

Factional struggle *for power among the new leaders* is *almost* a certainty, ***though*** *there will be an interval of superficial unity while each man consolidates his position.*

在新的領袖中，派系的權力鬥爭幾乎是必然的事，雖然當每個領袖在鞏固他的地位時，都會有片刻的團結。

factional ('fækʃənl̩) *adj.* 派系的　　struggle ('strʌgl̩) *n.* 鬥爭
certainty ('sɝtn̩tɪ) *n.* 必然的事
interval ('ɪntɚvl̩) *n.* （時間的）間隔
superficial (ˌsupɚ'fɪʃəl) *adj.* 表面的
unity ('junətɪ) *n.* 統一；團結
consolidate (kən'sɑləˌdet) *v.* 鞏固
position (pə'zɪʃən) *n.* 地位

The Chinese people will continue to stand *on the sidelines, allowed to speak only with an affirmative voice.*

中國人民將繼續當個旁觀者，只被容許表達肯定的意見。

> sideline (ˈsaɪd,laɪn) *n.* （球場的）邊線
> *on the sidelines* 當旁觀者；當局外人
> affirmative (əˈfɝmətɪv) *adj.* 肯定的
> voice (vɔɪs) *n.* 聲音；（表達出的）意見

1. (**C**) 共產黨
   (A) 一直努力想要停止他們搖擺不定的工作。
   (B) 似乎正熱烈活動中。
   (C) 總是在改變他們的政策。
   (D) 想要堅持穩定的措施。

   * *in full swing* 熱烈地進行   *adhere to* 堅持；固守
   steady (ˈstɛdɪ) *adj.* 穩定的   measure (ˈmɛʒɚ) *n.* 措施

2. (**D**) 根據這段文章，我們知道
   (A) 作者認為政策應該改變。
   (B) 作者希望能簡單地統一。
   (C) 作者贊成毛澤東的統治方式。
   (D) 作者比較喜歡以法律為基礎的政治制度。

3. (**B**) 根據本文，我們可以斷定
   (A) 新領袖應該努力爭取權力。
   (B) 未來的路線應該是穩定而且是可以預料的。
   (C) 中國人應該只被允許稱讚政府當局。
   (D) 中國人不該參與制定政府的政策。

   * conclude (kənˈklud) *v.* 斷定
   strive (straɪv) *v.* 努力
   predictable (prɪˈdɪktəbḷ) *adj.* 可預測的
   speak well of 稱讚
   authorities (əˈθɔrətɪz) *n.pl.* 當局   *take part in* 參與

4. (**A**) 「表面的」和 _____ 同義。

(A) 膚淺的　　　　　　　　(B) 胡亂的

(C) 人造的　　　　　　　　(D) 極好的

* synonymous (sɪˋnɑnəməs) *adj.* 同義的
  shallow (ˋʃælo) *adj.* 膚淺的
  artificial (ˏɑrtəˋfɪʃəl) *adj.* 人造的
  superb (suˋpɝb) *adj.* 極好的

5. (**B**) 本文的作者

(A) 希望每位領導者都能鞏固其地位。

(B) 反對派系鬥爭。

(C) 認為毛澤東用適當的方式運用他的權力，希望他能回來統治中國。

(D) 希望中國人民能全體一致地對政策表示贊同。

* strengthen (ˋstrɛŋθən) *v.* 使堅固；強化
  be opposed to 反對　　　proper (ˋprɑpɚ) *adj.* 適當的
  approval (əˋpruvl̩) *n.* 贊成
  unanimously (juˋnænəməslɪ) *adv.* 全體一致地

> 做英文閱讀測驗，是增加單字、複習單字的最好方法。

TEST 9

Read the following passage, and choose the best answer for each question.

Specialists in marketing have studied how to make people buy more food in a supermarket. They do all kinds of things that you do not even notice. For example, the simple, ordinary food that everybody must buy, like bread, milk, flour, and vegetable oil, is spread all over the store. You have to walk by all the more interesting — and more expensive — things in order to find what you need. The more expensive food is in packages with brightly-colored pictures. This food is placed at eye level so you see it and want to buy it. The things that you have to buy anyway are usually located on a higher or lower shelf. However, candy and other things that children like are on lower shelves. One study showed that when a supermarket moved four products from floor to eye level, it sold 78 percent more.

1. In a supermarket the simple and ordinary food is _____
   (A) placed at eye level.
   (B) placed on a higher shelf.
   (C) located on a lower shelf.
   (D) spread all over the store.

2. Packages that have brightly-colored pictures are _____

   (A) the more expensive food.

   (B) cheap food.

   (C) ordinary food.

   (D) children's food.

3. Children can find candy and other things they like _____

   (A) on lower shelves.

   (B) on higher shelves.

   (C) on lower and higher shelves.

   (D) at eye level.

4. A supermarket can increase sales by _____

   (A) selling more expensive products.

   (B) moving products from floor to eye level.

   (C) packing goods brightly.

   (D) cheating customers.

5. Specialists in marketing know a lot about _____

   (A) consumer psychology.

   (B) consumers' eyesight.

   (C) consumers' purchasing power.

   (D) the art of packaging.

TEST 9 詳解

Specialists *in marketing* have studied ***how** to make people buy more food in a supermarket*. They do all kinds of things *that you do not even notice*. *For example*, the simple, ordinary food *that everybody must buy, like bread, milk, flour, and vegetable oil*, is spread *all over the store*. You have to walk by all the *more* interesting — and *more* expensive — things *in order to find **what** you need*.

　　行銷專家研究過,如何才能使人們在超級市場中買更多的食物。他們做了各種一般人察覺不到的事。例如,每個人都要買的簡單普通的食物,像是麵包、牛奶、麵粉和蔬菜油,就被散布在商店的各個角落。要買到你需要的東西,就必須走過比較有趣,而且也比較貴的東西。

specialist (ˈspɛʃəlɪst) *n.* 專家　　marketing (ˈmɑrkɪtɪŋ) *n.* 行銷
ordinary (ˈɔrdṇˌɛrɪ) *adj.* 普通的　　flour (flaur) *n.* 麵粉

The *more* expensive food is in packages *with brightly-colored pictures*. This food is placed *at eye level* *so* you see it and want to buy it. The things ***that** you have to buy anyway* are usually located *on a higher or lower shelf*.

比較貴的食物,會用有鮮豔圖案的包裝。這種食物會放在你眼睛可平視的高度,讓你看到,並且想買。那些反正你一定得買的東西,通常就放在較高,或較低的架子上。

package (ˈpækɪdʒ) *n.* 包裝袋　　*eye level* 眼睛平視的高度
locate (loˈket) *v.* 使位於　　shelf (ʃɛlf) *n.* 架子

However, candy and other things *that children like* are on lower shelves. One study showed *that when* a supermarket moved four *products from floor to eye level*, it sold 78 percent more.

然而，小孩喜歡的糖果和其他東西，都擺在較低的架子上。有一項研究顯示，當超市將四項產品，由地板移至眼睛能平視的高度時，其銷售量便增加了百分之七十八。

1. (**D**) 在超級市場中，簡單且普通的食物
  (A) 被放在眼睛能平視的高度。 (B) 被放在較高的架子上。
  (C) 位於較低的架子上。   (D) <u>散布在商店的各個角落。</u>

2. (**A**) 使用有鮮豔圖案的包裝的是
  (A) <u>較貴的食物。</u>   (B) 便宜的食物。
  (C) 普通的食物。   (D) 小孩的食物。

3. (**A**) 小孩可以在 ＿＿＿＿＿＿＿ 找到自己喜歡的糖果和其他東西。
  (A) <u>較低的架子</u>   (B) 較高的架子
  (C) 較高與較低的架子 (D) 眼睛能平視的高度

4. (**B**) 超級市場可藉由 ＿＿＿＿＿＿＿ 增加其銷售量。
  (A) 賣更多昂貴的產品
  (B) <u>將商品由地板移至眼睛可平視的高度</u>
  (C) 將商品包裝得很鮮豔
  (D) 欺騙顧客
  * pack〔pæk〕*v.* 包裝（= *package*） goods〔gʊdz〕*n. pl.* 商品
  brightly〔'braɪtlɪ〕*adv.* 鮮豔地 customer〔'kʌstəmɚ〕*n.* 顧客

5. (**A**) 行銷專家很清楚
  (A) <u>消費者的心理。</u>   (B) 消費者的視力。
  (C) 消費者的購買力。 (D) 包裝的藝術。
  * consumer〔kən'sumɚ〕*n.* 消費者 purchase〔'pɝtʃəs〕*v.* 購買

TEST 10

Refer to the following telephone listing:

Lads and Lassies Play School	
2902 N.W. 22nd Place	375-7742
Land Clearing Service	
RFD Millville	462-1606
Lannon's Real Estate	
905 S.E. 2nd Terrace	372-9636
Larry's Pools Inc.	
4100 Oak Street	377-4276
London Recreation Club	
214 S. 33rd Drive	378-8432

1. Which number would you call if you wanted to play tennis?
    (A) 372-9636.   (B) 375-7742.
    (C) 378-8432.   (D) 377-4276.

2. Which number would you call if you were looking for a house or an apartment?
    (A) 375-7742.   (B) 372-9636.
    (C) 462-1606.   (D) 378-8432.

3. Which number would you call to find a place to leave your children?

   (A) 378-8432. (B) 375-7742.
   (C) 377-4276. (D) 462-1606.

4. Which number is most likely not a local number?

   (A) 375-7742. (B) 378-8432.
   (C) 462-1606. (D) 372-9636.

5. Which number would you call for swimming equipment?

   (A) 375-7742. (B) 378-8432.
   (C) 377-4276. (D) 372-9636.

TEST 10 詳解

參考下列電話一覽表：

青少年遊樂學校
    2902 N.W. 22nd Place（地址）   375-7742

整地服務社
    RFD Millville（地址）   462-1606

藍農房地產公司
    905 S.E. 2nd Terrace（地址）   372-9636

拉利游泳器具有限公司
    4100 Oak Street（地址）   377-4276

倫敦娛樂俱樂部
    214 S. 33rd Drive（地址）   378-8432

lad〔læd〕*n.* 少年   lassie〔'læsɪ〕*n.* 少女
real estate 房地產
incorporated〔ɪn'kɔrpə,retɪd〕*adj.* 有限責任的（簡寫 Inc. 附於公司名稱之後）
recreation〔,rikrɪ'eʃən〕*n.* 娛樂

1. (**C**) 如果你想打網球，你要打幾號電話？
    (A) 372-9636。   (B) 375-7742。
    (C) 378-8432。   (D) 377-4276。

2. (**B**) 如果你在找房子或公寓，你要打幾號電話？
    (A) 375-7742。   (B) 372-9636。
    (C) 462-1606。   (D) 378-8432。

3. (**B**) 你要打幾號電話，可以找到照顧你孩子的地方？

　　　(A) 378-8432。　　　　　　(B) <u>375-7742</u>。

　　　(C) 377-4276。　　　　　　(D) 462-1606。

4. (**C**) 哪一個最不可能是當地的電話號碼？

　　　(A) 375-7742。　　　　　　(B) 378-8432。

　　　(C) <u>462-1606</u>。　　　　　　(D) 372-9636。

5. (**C**) 你要打幾號電話，可以買到游泳器具？

　　　(A) 375-7742。　　　　　　(B) 378-8432。

　　　(C) <u>377-4276</u>。　　　　　　(D) 372-9636。

> 答題時，先將明顯的錯誤答案刪去，如果能刪
> 掉三個一定錯誤的答案，剩下的答案，即使沒
> 有把握，也是正確答案。

TEST 11

Read the following passage, and choose the best answer for each question.

Why do people take part in such a risky activity as bungee jumping? They jump from a high place (perhaps a bridge or a hot-air balloon) 200 meters above the ground with an elastic rope tied to their ankles. According to psychologists, it is because life in modern societies has become safe and boring. Not very long ago, people's lives were constantly under threat. They had to go out and hunt for food, diseases could not easily be cured, and life was a continuous battle for survival. Nowadays, according to many people, life offers little excitement. They live and work in comparatively safe environments; they buy food in shops; and there are doctors and hospitals to look after them if they become ill. The answer for some of these people is to seek danger in activities such as bungee jumping.

1. In bungee jumping, people _____
   (A) jump as high as they can.
   (B) slide down a rope to the ground.
   (C) attach a rope and fall to the ground.
   (D) fall towards the ground without a rope.

2. People probably take part in dangerous sports nowadays
   because _____

   (A) they have a lot of free time.
   (B) they can go to hospital if they are injured.
   (C) their lives lack excitement.
   (D) they no longer need to hunt for food.

3. The place which is not suitable for bungee jumping
   is _____

   (A) a bridge two hundred meters high.
   (B) a cliff.
   (C) a hot-air balloon.
   (D) a five-story building.

4. If we were living in ancient times now, _____

   (A) we would have to hunt for food.
   (B) we could buy food in shops.
   (C) we would have doctors to look after our health.
   (D) we would have little excitement.

5. Life in the past was basically a continuous battle
   for _____

   (A) fame.   (B) wealth.
   (C) survival.   (D) power.

TEST 11 詳解

Why do people take part in such a risky activity as bungee jumping? They jump *from a high place (perhaps a bridge or a hot-air balloon) 200 meters above the ground with an elastic rope tied to their ankles*.

　　爲什麼人們要參加像是高空彈跳這麼危險的活動呢？他們會在腳踝上綁上有彈性的繩子，然後從離地面二百公尺高的地方（也許是一座橋，或是熱氣球上）跳下來。

　　risky〔'rɪskɪ〕 *adj.* 危險的　　***bungee jumping*** 高空彈跳
　　balloon〔bə'lun〕 *n.* 氣球　　　***hot-air balloon*** 熱氣球
　　elastic〔ɪ'læstɪk〕 *adj.* 有彈性的　　ankle〔'æŋkl̩〕 *n.* 腳踝

According to psychologists, it is ***because*** life in modern societies has become safe and boring. *Not very long ago*, people's lives were *constantly* under threat. They had to go out ***and*** hunt for food, diseases could not *easily* be cured, ***and*** life was a continuous battle *for survival*.

根據心理學家的說法，這是因爲現代人的生活，已變得旣安全而且無聊。不久以前，人們的生命會不斷受到威脅。他們必須出去找食物，生病也不容易治好，生活是一場不斷求生存的戰爭。

　　threat〔θrɛt〕 *n.* 威脅
　　hunt for 尋找　　battle〔'bætl̩〕 *n.* 戰爭
　　survival〔sə'vaɪvl̩〕 *n.* 生存

Nowadays, according to many people, life offers little excitement. They live and work *in comparatively safe environments*; they buy food *in shops*; *and* there are doctors and hospitals to look after them *if they become ill.* The answer *for some of these people* is to seek danger *in activities such as bungee jumping.*

現在，根據許多人的說法，生活所提供的刺激太少了。人們在比較安全的環境中生活與工作；在商店裏買食物；如果生病了，有醫生和醫院照顧。對於其中的一些人而言，解決之道就是，在像是高空彈跳這類的活動中尋求危險。

comparatively (kəm'pærətɪvlɪ) *adv.* 比較上而言

1. (**C**) 高空彈跳時，人們
   (A) 儘可能跳高一點。　　　(B) 利用繩子向下滑到地上。
   (C) 綁條繩子，往地上跳。　(D) 不用繩子就往地上跳。
   * slide (slaɪd) *v.* 滑行　　attach (ə'tætʃ) *v.* 繫上；綁上

2. (**C**) 現在人們可能會參加危險的運動，那是因為
   (A) 他們有許多空閒時間。　(B) 如果受傷可以去醫院。
   (C) 生活缺少刺激。　　　　(D) 他們不再需要尋找食物。

3. (**D**) 不適合高空彈跳的地方是
   (A) 兩百公尺高的橋。　　　(B) 懸崖。
   (C) 熱氣球。　　　　　　　(D) 五層樓高的建築物。

4. (**A**) 如果現在我們生活在古代，
   (A) 我們就必須去尋找食物。　(B) 我們可以在商店中買食物。
   (C) 我們有醫生來照顧我們的健康。　(D) 我們就沒有什麼刺激。

5. (**C**) 在過去，生活基本上是一場不斷求 ＿＿＿＿＿＿ 的戰爭。
   (A) 名聲　　　　　　　　　(B) 財富
   (C) 生存　　　　　　　　　(D) 權力

TEST 12

Read the following passage, and choose the best answer for each question.

The executive branch of the American government puts the country's laws into effect. The president of the United States is a member of the executive branch. The president must be at least 35 years old, and be a natural citizen of the United States. In addition, he must have lived in the United States for at least 14 years, and be a civilian. The president is elected every four years and can not serve more than two terms in a row. The vice president acts as president of the Senate. When the president receives a bill from Congress, he must sign it in order for it to become a law. However, if he disagrees with the law, he can veto, or reject, it. The president can also ask the Congress to declare war. He also appoints the justices to the Supreme Court. He must do his job according to the Constitution, or he may be impeached, that is, charged with a crime by Congress. The executive branch is a very important part of the U.S. government and must work with the other two branches, i.e., the judicial branch and the legislative branch, according to the Constitution.

1. The president of the United States must be _____
   - (A) no more than 35.
   - (B) under 35.
   - (C) at least 35.
   - (D) over 49.

2. In the States, the presidential election takes place _____

   - (A) every six years.
   - (B) every five years.
   - (C) every four years.
   - (D) every other year.

3. According to the Constitution, the Congress can _____
   - (A) impeach the president if he acts against the law.
   - (B) appoint the justices to the Supreme Court.
   - (C) act as the president of the Senate.
   - (D) not declare war against another country.

4. The president of the United States must be _____
   - (A) a naturalized citizen.
   - (B) a natural citizen.
   - (C) a civilized person.
   - (D) a judge.

5. The American government is mainly made up of _____
   - (A) two branches.
   - (B) three branches.
   - (C) four branches.
   - (D) five branches.

TEST 12 詳解

The executive branch *of the American government* puts the country's laws into effect.

美國政府的行政主管部門，負責使國家的法律生效。

executive (ɪgˋzɛkjutɪv) *adj.* 行政的　　branch (bræntʃ) *n.* 分部；部門
put ~ into effect 實行 ~；使 ~ 生效

The president *of the United States* is a member *of the executive branch*. The president must be at least 35 years old, *and* be a natural citizen *of the United States*. *In addition*, he must have lived *in the United States for at least 14 years*, *and* be a civilian. The president is elected *every four years and* can not serve more than two terms *in a row*.

美國總統是行政主管部門中的一員。總統必須年滿三十五歲，而且是生來就有美國國籍的公民。此外，他還必須是在美國居住滿十四年以上的平民。總統每四年選一次，而且不得連續擔任兩任以上。

at least 至少
natural citizen 生來就具有該國國籍的公民 (= *natural-born citizen*)
civilian (sɪˋvɪljən) *n.* 平民 (與軍、警、政府官員等相對)
elect (ɪˋlɛkt) *v.* 選舉；選出
serve (sɝv) *v.* 任職　　term (tɝm) *n.* 任期
in a row 連續地

The vice president acts as president *of the Senate*. ***When the***

president receives a bill from Congress, he must sign it *in order*

for it to become a law. However, ***if he disagrees with the law***,

he can veto, ***or*** reject, it.

副總統是參議院的議長。當總統收到來自國會的法案，必須簽署後，才能成爲
法律。然而，如果他不同意，他可以否決，也就是駁回這項法案。

> ***vice president*** 副總統　　***act as*** 擔任
> president ('prɛzədənt) *n.* 議長　　Senate ('sɛnɪt) *n.* 參議院
> bill (bɪl) *n.* 法案　　Congress ('kɑŋgrəs) *n.* 國會
> veto ('vito) *v.* 否決　　reject (rɪ'dʒɛkt) *v.* 不受理；駁回

The president can *also* ask the Congress to declare war. He

also appoints the justices *to the Supreme Court*. He must do his

job *according to the Constitution*, ***or*** he may be impeached, *that*

is, charged with a crime *by Congress*.

總統也可以要求國會宣戰。他也可以指派最高法院的法官。總統必須依據憲法
行事，否則就可能被彈劾，也就是被國會指控有罪。

> declare (dɪ'klɛr) *v.* 宣布　　appoint (ə'pɔɪnt) *v.* 指派；任命
> justice ('dʒʌstɪs) *n.* 法官 (= *judge*)
> supreme (sə'prim) *adj.* 最高權威的　　***the Supreme Court*** 最高法院
> constitution (,kɑnstə'tjuʃən) *n.* 憲法
> impeach (ɪm'pitʃ) *v.* 彈劾　　***that is*** 也就是
> charge (tʃɑrdʒ) *v.* 控告　　crime (kraɪm) *n.* 罪

The executive branch is a *very* important part *of the U.S.*

government **and** must work *with the other two branches, i.e., the*

judicial branch and the legislative branch, according to the

Constitution.

行政主管部門是美國政府非常重要的一個部門，而且根據憲法，必須和其他兩個部門合作，也就是司法與立法部門。

> i.e. ('aɪ'i) *adj.* 也就是 (= *that is* = *that is to say*)
> judicial (dʒu'dɪʃəl) *adj.* 司法的
> legislative ('lɛdʒɪs,letɪv) *adj.* 立法的

1. (**C**) 美國總統必須

    (A) 不超過三十五歲。   (B) 三十五歲以下。

    (C) <u>至少三十五歲。</u>   (D) 四十九歲以上。

2. (**C**) 在美國，總統選舉 _____ 舉行一次。

    (A) 每六年   (B) 每五年

    (C) <u>每四年</u>   (D) 每隔一年

3. (**A**) 根據憲法，

    (A) <u>如果總統有違法的行為，國會可以彈劾總統。</u>

    (B) 國會可以指派最高法院的法官。

    (C) 國會可以擔任參議院的議長。

    (D) 國會不能向另一國宣戰。

    * *act against*~ 行為違反~

4. (**B**) 美國總統必須是

(A) 入美國國籍的公民。

(B) <u>天生具有美國國籍的公民。</u>

(C) 文明人。

(D) 法官。

* naturalize (ˈnætʃərəlˌaɪz) *v.* 使歸化；使入籍

civilized (ˈsɪvlˌaɪzd) *adj.* 文明的

5. (**B**) 美國政府主要是由 _____ 所組成。

(A) 兩個主管部門   (B) <u>三個主管部門</u>

(C) 四個主管部門   (D) 五個主管部門

* mainly (ˈmenlɪ) *adv.* 主要地

be made up of 由～組成

「劉毅英文家教班」模考試題的格式、字體大小、版面編排，和真正試題相同。同學只要將劉英文的講義當課本一樣，每天朗讀，「學科能力測驗」自然拿高分。

TEST 13

Read the following passage, and choose the best answer for each question.

According to news reports, drunk driving has become increasingly common over the past few years. It is time for the authorities to assume a truly tough stance toward this dangerous act. Driving under the influence of alcohol is even more dangerous than speeding and running a red light. A driver who is drunk can lose control of his or her vehicle suddenly and hit any pedestrians and automobiles on the road that happen to be in his path, and the result is usually a fatal tragedy. Car ownership has increased rapidly in recent years because of elevated living standards. And drinking is an addiction among a growing number of the island's residents. These trends have combined to make drunk driving widespread. The only effective way to reduce drunk driving is to make the laws stiffer and enforce them more strictly.

1. Drunk driving usually results in _____
    (A) comedy.
    (B) tragedy.
    (C) law-abiding acts.
    (D) control of one's vehicle.

2. A drunken driver is unable to keep his car under control because of the influence of _____
   (A) pedestrians.   (B) alcohol.
   (C) laws.   (D) reports.

3. The rise of living standards has enabled more and more people to _____
   (A) run a red light.
   (B) be addicted to drunk driving.
   (C) own private cars.
   (D) control their vehicles well.

4. The only effective way to reduce drunk driving is to _____
   (A) take weak measures against drunken drivers.
   (B) enforce laws more strictly.
   (C) build better roads.
   (D) stop stores from selling wines.

5. In comparison with speeding and running a red light, drunk driving _____
   (A) requires more driving skills.
   (B) is a more dangerous act.
   (C) is scarcely seen.
   (D) does not endanger pedestrians.

TEST 13 詳解

According to news reports, drunk driving has become *increasingly* common *over the past few years*. It is time *for the authorities* to assume a *truly* tough stance *toward this dangerous act*.

根據新聞報導，在過去幾年，酒醉駕駛已變得愈來愈普遍。該是政府當局，對這項危險行為，採取真正強硬態度的時候了。

> ***drunk driving*** 酒醉駕駛
> increasingly (ɪnˈkrisɪŋlɪ) *adv.* 愈來愈
> authorities (əˈθɔrətɪz) *n.pl.* 當局
> assume (əˈsjum) *v.* 採取
> tough (tʌf) *adj.* 強硬的
> stance (stæns) *n.* 態度　　act (ækt) *n.* 行為

Driving *under the influence of alcohol* is *even more* dangerous *than* speeding and running a red light. A driver *who is drunk* can lose control *of his or her vehicle suddenly and* hit any pedestrians and automobiles *on the road that happen to be in his path, and* the result is *usually* a fatal tragedy.

在酒精的影響之下開車，甚至比超速和闖紅燈還要危險。酒醉的駕駛人會突然失去對車輛的控制，因而撞到碰巧在其行進路線的行人和汽車，而結果通常是致命的悲劇。

alcohol ('ælkə,hɔl) *n.* 酒精　　speeding ('spidɪŋ) *n.* 超速
run a red light 闖紅燈　　vehicle ('viɪkl̩) *n.* 車輛
pedestrian (pə'dɛstrɪən) *n.* 行人
automobile (,ɔtəmə'bil) *n.* 汽車
happen to 碰巧　　path (pæθ) *n.* 行進路線
fatal ('fetl̩) *adj.* 致命的
tragedy ('trædʒədɪ) *n.* 悲劇

Car ownership has increased *rapidly in recent years because of elevated living standards*. ***And*** drinking is an addiction *among a growing number of the island's residents*. These trends have combined to make drunk driving widespread.

近年來，由於生活水準提高，擁有汽車的人數，增加得十分迅速。而台灣的居民，也愈來愈多人有酒癮。這些趨勢結合起來，使得酒醉駕車變得十分普遍。

ownership ('onɚ,ʃɪp) *n.* 所有 (權)；擁有
recent ('risn̩t) *adj.* 最近的
elevated ('ɛlə,vetɪd) *adj.* 提高的
living standard 生活水準
addiction (ə'dɪkʃən) *n.* 沈迷；癮
growing ('groɪŋ) *adj.* 日益增加的
resident ('rɛzədənt) *n.* 居民
trend (trɛnd) *n.* 趨勢　　combine (kəm'baɪn) *v.* 結合
widespread ('waɪd'sprɛd) *adj.* 普遍的

The only effective way *to reduce drunk driving* is to make the laws stiffer ***and*** enforce them *more strictly*.

要減少酒醉駕車，唯一有效的方法，就是制定更嚴格的法律，並且嚴加執行。

> effective〔ə'fɛktɪv〕*adj.* 有效的
> stiff〔stɪf〕*adj.* 嚴厲的
> enforce〔ɪn'fors〕*v.* 強制執行
> strictly〔'strɪktlɪ〕*adv.* 嚴格地

1. (**B**) 酒醉駕駛通常會造成

   (A) 喜劇。　　　　　　　　　(B) 悲劇。

   (C) 守法的行爲。　　　　　　(D) 控制一個人的車輛。

   > * comedy〔'kɑmədɪ〕*n.* 喜劇
   >   law-abiding〔'lɔə,baɪdɪŋ〕*adj.* 守法的

2. (**B**) 酒醉駕車的人無法控制車，那是因爲他會受到 _____ 的
   影響。

   (A) 行人　　　　　　　　　　(B) 酒精

   (C) 法律　　　　　　　　　　(D) 報導

3. (**C**) 生活水準的提高，使得愈來愈多的人能夠

   (A) 闖紅燈。

   (B) 沈迷於酒醉駕車。

   (C) 擁有自己的車。

   (D) 將車輛控制得很好。

   > * rise〔raɪz〕*n.* 上升；提高　　enable〔ɪn'ebḷ〕*v.* 使能夠
   >   ***be addicted to*** 沈迷於
   >   private〔'praɪvɪt〕*adj.* 私人的

4. (**B**) 要減少酒醉駕駛，唯一有效的方法是

   (A) 對酒醉駕駛的人採取軟弱的措施。

   (B) 更嚴格地執行法律。

   (C) 建造更好的道路。

   (D) 禁止商店賣酒。

   * measure (ˈmɛʒɚ) *n.* 措施
   take~measures 採取~措施　　*stop~from* 阻止~

5. (**B**) 比起超速與闖紅燈，酒醉駕駛

   (A) 需要更多的駕駛技術。

   (B) 是種更危險的行為。

   (C) 很少見。

   (D) 並不會危害到行人。

   * comparison (kəmˈpærəsn̩) *n.* 比較
   require (rɪˈkwaɪr) *v.* 需要
   in comparison with 與~相比
   scarcely (ˈskɛrslɪ) *adv.* 幾乎不
   endanger (ɪnˈdendʒɚ) *v.* 危害

書中有問題不懂，可至：台北市重慶南路
一段 10 號 7 樓，找劉毅老師。

TEST 14

Read the following passage, and choose the best answer for each question.

I am more of a host than a guest. I like people to stay with me but do not much care for staying with them, and usually say I am too busy. The only people we ask to stay with us are people we like — I do not believe in business hospitality, which has the seed of corruption in it — and every Friday I work in a pleasant glow just because I know some nice people are coming down by the last train. I am genuinely glad to see them. But I suspect that I am still more delighted when they go, and the house is ours again.

1. Often on Fridays, the writer will be _____
   (A) anticipating the arrival of his guests.
   (B) ready to retire for the weekend.
   (C) sending out invitations.
   (D) prepared to start working again.

2. All things considered, the writer _____
   (A) enjoys the company of business associates more than personal friends.
   (B) is a great host, to whose parties many celebrities come.
   (C) would rather be left alone to the peace and quiet of his home.
   (D) might yet prove himself to be a better guest than a generous host.

3. When turning down a friend's invitation, the writer will say, ―――――――
   - (A) "I am more of a host."
   - (B) "I am not much of a guest."
   - (C) "I do not much care."
   - (D) "My time is fully employed."

4. The writer does not consider business entertainment worth his while because ―――――――
   - (A) he does not like his business friends.
   - (B) he does not think they are pleasant companions.
   - (C) he suspects there is a dishonest motive.
   - (D) business friends are mostly corrupt.

5. The writer probably lives ―――――――
   - (A) in the city.
   - (B) in the country.
   - (C) in a foreign country.
   - (D) within a short walk from his office.

TEST 14 詳解

I am more of a host ***than*** *a guest*. I like people to stay with me ***but*** do not *much* care for staying with them, ***and*** *usually* say I am *too busy*.

與其說我是個客人，不如說我是個主人。我喜歡別人和我在一起，但卻不怎麼喜歡和他們在一起，而我通常說我太忙了。

> ***more*** A ***than*** B　與其說是 A，不如說是 B（詳見文法寶典 p.201）
> ***care for*** 喜歡

The only people *we ask to stay with us* are people *we like* — I do not believe in business hospitality, ***which*** *has the seed of corruption in it* — ***and*** *every Friday* I work *in a pleasant glow* just ***because*** *I know some nice people are coming down by the last train.*

我們唯一會要求和我們在一起的，是我們所喜歡的人 —— 我不相信應酬是有益的，因為那是墮落的根源 —— 所有的禮拜五，我都很愉快地工作，只因為我知道，有一些很好的人要搭最後一班火車來。

> * we ask to stay with us 和 we like 是省略了 that 的形容詞子句，分別修飾其先行詞 people。which…it 是補述用法的形容詞子句，修飾 hospitality。in a pleasant glow 是副詞片語，修飾 work。because …train 是副詞子句，修飾 work。
>
> | | |
> |---|---|
> | ***believe in*** 相信～是好的 | hospitality〔͵hɑspɪˈtælətɪ〕*n.* 慇懃款待 |
> | seed〔sid〕*n.* 種子；根源 | corruption〔kəˈrʌpʃən〕*n.* 墮落 |
> | glow〔glo〕*n.* 興高采烈 | |

I am *genuinely* glad to see them. ***But*** I suspect ***that*** *I am still more delighted* ***when*** *they go,* ***and*** *the house is ours again.*

我真的很高興看見他們。但我認爲,當他們走了,房子又屬於我們自己的時候,我會更快樂。

　　genuinely〔'dʒɛnjʊɪnlɪ〕*adv.* 真正地　　suspect〔sə'spɛkt〕*v.* 懷疑;認爲

1.(**A**) 通常在星期五,作者會

　　(A) 期待他客人的到來。　　　(B) 準備離開去度週末。
　　(C) 寄出邀請函。　　　　　　(D) 準備又要開始工作。

　　* anticipate〔æn'tɪsə,pet〕*v.* 期待　　retire〔rɪ'taɪr〕*v.* 離去
　　invitation〔,ɪnvə'teʃən〕*n.* 邀請函

2.(**C**) 綜觀各種情況,作者

　　(A) 喜歡和生意上的夥伴在一起,甚於自己的朋友。
　　(B) 是個很棒的主人,他的宴會有很多名人參加。
　　(C) 寧願獨處,享受自己家中的安詳與寧靜。
　　(D) 可能仍會證明自己是個較好的客人,而不是慷慨的主人。

　　* *all things considered* 綜觀各種情況　　associate〔ə'soʃɪɪt〕*n.* 夥伴
　　celebrity〔sə'lɛbrətɪ〕*n.* 名人　　quiet〔'kwaɪət〕*n.* 寧靜

3.(**D**) 作者拒絕朋友的邀請時,會說:

　　(A)「我比較像是個主人。」　　(B)「我不怎麼是個客人。」
　　(C)「我不怎麼在乎。」　　　　(D)「我的時間都排滿了。」

　　* *turn down* 拒絕　　employ〔ɪm'plɔɪ〕*v.* 使用

4.(**C**) 作者認爲不值得去應酬,是因爲

　　(A) 他不喜歡生意上的朋友。　　(B) 他認爲他們不是令人愉快的同伴。
　　(C) 他懷疑會有不誠實的動機。　(D) 生意上的朋友大多很墮落。

　　* *be worth one's while* 值得(某人)做　　motive〔'motɪv〕*n.* 動機

5.(**B**) 作者可能住在

　　(A) 城市。　　　　　　　　　(B) 鄉下。
　　(C) 國外。　　　　　　　　　(D) 離他辦公室很近的地方。

　　* walk〔wɔk〕*n.* 走路的距離

TEST 15

Read the following passage, and choose the best answer for each question.

POPULATION CHANGES —
RECENT CENSUS STATISTICS

	1990	2000
Oak Hill		34,510
		34,265
Holly		19,451
		10,900
Avondale	6,782	
		15,943
Beechwood	7,569	
	7,620	
Lakeside	1,243	
	998	

1. Which of the following cities increased its population considerably during the ten-year period?

   (A) Avondale.   (B) Beechwood.
   (C) Oak Hill.   (D) Holly.

2. Which city showed the most appreciable decrease in population in the ten-year period?

   (A) Beechwood.   (B) Oak Hill.
   (C) Holly.   (D) Lakeside.

3. Which city's population decreased by the smallest percentage?

    (A) Holly.   (B) Lakeside.

    (C) Beechwood.   (D) Oak Hill.

4. Which city had no population increase or decrease?

    (A) Oak Hill.   (B) Lakeside.

    (C) Beechwood.   (D) None of the above.

5. If someone wants to start his own service business, which city will probably offer the best opportunities for success?

    (A) Oak Hill.   (B) Beechwood.

    (C) Holly.   (D) Lakeside.

TEST 15 詳解

人 口 變 更 ——
最近人口調查統計表

	虛線代表 1990	實線代表 2000
橡 山 市	·································· 34,510	———————— 34,265
赫 利 市	·················· 19,451	——— 10,900
愛旺德爾市	······ 6,782	——————— 15,943
山毛櫸市	········· 7,569	——— 7,620
湖 濱 市	···· 1,243	— 998

recent〔'risn̩t〕*adj.* 最近的　　census〔'sɛnsəs〕*n.* 人口調查
statistics〔stə'tɪstɪks〕*n.* 統計表　　beech〔bitʃ〕*n.* 山毛櫸

1.(**A**) 下列的城市中，哪一個在十年間人口增加很多？
(A) 愛旺德爾市。　　　　　　(B) 山毛櫸市。
(C) 橡山市。　　　　　　　　(D) 赫利市。
* considerably〔kən'sɪdərəblɪ〕*adv.* 相當大地

2.(**C**) 下列哪一個城市，在十年間人口減少最明顯？
(A) 山毛櫸市。　　　　　　　(B) 橡山市。
(C) 赫利市。　　　　　　　　(D) 湖濱市。
* appreciable〔ə'priʃɪəbl̩〕*adj.* 可察覺的；相當多的

3. (**D**) 哪一個城市人口減少的百分比最小？

　　(A) 赫利市。　　　　　　　　(B) 湖濱市。
　　(C) 山毛櫸市。　　　　　　　(D) 橡山市。

　　* percentage (pɚ'sɛntɪdʒ) n. 百分比

4. (**D**) 哪一個都市的人口既沒增加也沒減少？

　　(A) 橡山市。　　　　　　　　(B) 湖濱市。
　　(C) 山毛櫸市。　　　　　　　(D) 以上皆非。

5. (**A**) 如果有人想創立服務業，哪個都市能提供最佳的成功機會？

　　(A) 橡山市。　　　　　　　　(B) 山毛櫸市。
　　(C) 赫利市。　　　　　　　　(D) 湖濱市。

在考「學科能力測驗」的時候，可將試題中，
閱讀測驗的單字或片語圈出來，用在英文作文
中，但不能抄整句，以免被發現。

TEST 16

Read the following passage, and choose the best answer for each question.

The aye-aye is a rainforest animal. It eats insects which live under the bark of trees. It has very good ears. It's capable of hearing the slightest sound. It puts its ear next to the bark of a tree and listens for signs of movement. Then it quickly bites a hole in the bark and puts its middle finger into the hole to pull out the insect. It also uses its middle finger for combing its hair.

It lives only in Madagascar. It sleeps during the day and is active at night. It often hangs upside down from branches. And the strong claws on its feet are used as hooks. It is called "aye-aye" after the strange noises it makes, which are blown through its nose. The island people are frightened of the noises.

1. The aye-aye feeds on _____
   (A) barks.   (B) fruit.
   (C) insects.   (D) leaves.

2. The aye-aye lives in _____
   (A) trees.   (B) caves.
   (C) holes.   (D) many places.

3. The aye-aye gets its food with _____

    (A) its long tongue.
    (B) its middle finger.
    (C) the claws on its feet.
    (D) hooks.

4. Which statement about the aye-aye is wrong?

    (A) It sleeps during the day and is active at night.
    (B) It is called "aye-aye" because it makes strange noises "aye-aye".
    (C) The strange noises it makes are from its nose.
    (D) It has very good eyes so that it is active at night.

5. Madagascar is _____

    (A) a rainforest.
    (B) a kind of tree.
    (C) an island.
    (D) an insect.

TEST 16 詳解

The aye-aye is a rainforest animal. It eats insects *which live under the bark of trees*. It has *very* good ears. It's capable of hearing the slightest sound. It puts its ear *next to the bark of a tree* **and** listens for signs *of movement*. *Then* it *quickly* bites a hole *in the bark* **and** puts its middle finger *into the hole to pull out the insect*. It *also* uses its middle finger *for combing its hair*.

指猴是種熱帶雨林的動物。牠專門吃生長在樹皮裏的昆蟲。牠的耳朵非常靈敏，連最輕微的聲音都聽得見。指猴會將耳朵貼在樹皮上，聽看看裏面有無動靜。然後很快地在樹皮上挖個洞，將中指伸進洞裏，拉出昆蟲。牠也會用中指來梳一梳牠的毛髮。

> **aye-aye** (ˈaɪˌaɪ) *n.* 指猴（原產於非洲馬達加斯加島，淡黃色皮毛，大耳尖爪，夜間活動，常發出「唉，唉」的鳴聲。）
> **rainforest** (ˈrenˌfɔrɪst) *n.* 熱帶雨林
> **insect** (ˈɪnsɛkt) *n.* 昆蟲　　**bark** (bɑrk) *n.* 樹皮
> **sign** (saɪn) *n.* 跡象　　**comb** (kom) *v.* 梳（髮）；刷（毛）

It lives *only in Madagascar*. It sleeps *during the day* **and** is active *at night*. It *often* hangs *upside down from branches*. **And** the strong claws *on its feet* are used as hooks. It is called "aye-aye" *after the strange noises it makes*, **which** *are blown through its nose*. The island people are frightened of the noises.

　　指猴是馬達加斯加島的特產，是晝伏夜出的動物。牠常會倒掛在樹枝上，其腳上強有力的爪子，可用來當作鉤子。牠的名字叫 "aye-aye"，是因為牠會由鼻子發出奇怪的「唉，唉」聲。島上的居民很怕聽見這種聲音。

Madagascar〔͵mædə'gæskə〕n. 馬達加斯加島（非洲東南邊印度洋上的島嶼）
active〔'æktɪv〕adj. 活躍的　　*upside down* 上下顛倒地
hang upside down 倒掛著　　branch〔bræntʃ〕n. 樹枝
claw〔klɔ〕n. 爪子　　hook〔huk〕n. 鉤子
blow〔blo〕v. 吹氣　　frightened〔'fraɪtn̩d〕adj. 害怕的
be frightened of 害怕（= *be afraid of*）

1. (**C**) 指猴是以 ＿＿＿＿＿ 為食。

    (A) 樹皮　　(B) 水果　　(C) 昆蟲　　(D) 葉子

    * *feed on* 以～為食

2. (**A**) 指猴住在

    (A) 樹上。　(B) 洞穴裏。　(C) 洞裏。　(D) 很多地方。

    * cave〔kev〕n. 洞穴

3. (**B**) 指猴用 ＿＿＿＿＿ 來捕捉食物。

    (A) 長長的舌頭　　(B) 中指
    (C) 腳上的爪子　　(D) 鉤子

4. (**D**) 下列關於指猴的敘述，何者為非？

    (A) 牠晝伏夜出。
    (B) 牠被稱為 "aye-aye"，是因為牠會發出奇怪的「唉，唉」聲。
    (C) 牠是從鼻子發出怪聲音。
    (D) 牠的眼睛很好，所以才能晚上出來活動。

5. (**C**) 馬達加斯加是

    (A) 一片熱帶雨林。　　(B) 一種樹。
    (C) 一座島。　　　　　(D) 一種昆蟲。

TEST 17

Read the following passage, and choose the best answer for each question.

Brazilian food is like Brazil itself. It's a rich mixture of many things from many places. Some dishes are like Portuguese dishes because many Portuguese people went to live in Brazil. Other dishes are not like any European dishes. The flavors are special to Brazil. Brazilian cooks are lucky. They can get excellent fish from the ocean, and good meat from the farms. And they can get all kinds of tropical fruits and vegetables, which give Brazilian dishes their special delicious taste. Brazil is a large country. Each area has its own history and traditions, and so has its own way of cooking. If you are in Rio de Janeiro, you should try the "feijoada," a very rich mixture of different meats with black beans. Brazilians usually eat it on the weekend. It's not a dish to eat in a hurry.

1. The article is about _____
   (A) Brazilian cooks. (B) Brazil.
   (C) Brazilian food. (D) Brazilian history.

2. Brazilian food _____
   (A) is all the same.
   (B) is all like Portuguese food.
   (C) is a mixture of different foods.
   (D) has no special flavors.

3. The special taste of Brazilian food comes from _____

   (A) the ocean.

   (B) the farms.

   (C) tropical fruits and vegetables.

   (D) Portugal.

4. "Feijoada" is a dish very special to _____

   (A) Europe.

   (B) Portugal.

   (C) Brazil.

   (D) Rio de Janeiro.

5. Brazilians usually eat "feijoada" _____

   (A) on holidays.

   (B) on the weekend.

   (C) in a hurry.

   (D) at the beach.

TEST 17 詳解

Brazilian food is like Brazil itself. It's a rich mixture *of many things from many places*. Some dishes are like Portuguese dishes *because many Portuguese people went to live in Brazil*. Other dishes are not like any European dishes. The flavors are special to Brazil.

巴西的食物就像巴西本身一樣，是種來自各地的許多東西，十分豐富的混合。有些菜像葡萄牙菜，因為很多葡萄牙人來到巴西定居。而有些菜則和任何歐洲菜都不像，有巴西特有的風味。

> Brazilian〔brə'zɪljən〕*adj.* 巴西的　　Brazil〔brə'zɪl〕*n.* 巴西
> mixture〔'mɪkstʃ≈〕*n.* 混合
> Portuguese〔'portʃə,giz〕*adj.* 葡萄牙的　　flavor〔'flev≈〕*n.* 味道

Brazilian cooks are lucky. They can get excellent fish *from the ocean*, and good meat *from the farms*. *And* they can get all kinds of tropical fruits and vegetables, *which give Brazilian dishes their special delicious taste*.

巴西的廚師很幸運。他們可以得到來自大海很棒的魚，來自農場很好的肉，而且還有能使巴西菜既獨特又美味的各種熱帶水果和蔬菜。

> tropical〔'trɑpɪkḷ〕*adj.* 熱帶的　　taste〔test〕*n.* 味道

Brazil is a large country. Each area has its own history and traditions, ***and so*** has its own way *of cooking.* *If you are in Rio de Janeiro*, you should try the "feijoada," *a very rich mixture of different meats with black beans.* Brazilians *usually* eat it *on the weekend.* It's not a dish *to eat in a hurry.*

巴西是個幅員廣大的國家。每個地區都有自己的歷史和傳統，也有其獨特的烹調方式。如果你是在里約熱內盧，那就該嚐嚐 "feijoada"，這道菜十分豐富，混合了不同種類的肉和黑豆。巴西人通常會在週末吃這道菜。這道菜應該要慢慢品嚐。

> Rio de Janeiro (ˈriodədʒəˈnɪro) *n.* 里約熱內盧（位於巴西東南部的海港）
> bean (bin) *n.* 豆子

1. (**C**) 本文是談論關於
   (A) 巴西的廚師。　　　　(B) 巴西。
   (C) 巴西的食物。　　　　(D) 巴西的歷史。

2. (**C**) 巴西的食物
   (A) 都一樣。　　　　　　(B) 都像葡萄牙的食物。
   (C) 是不同食物的混合。　(D) 沒有特殊風味。

3. (**C**) 巴西食物的特殊風味是來自於
   (A) 海洋。　　　　　　　(B) 農莊。
   (C) 熱帶的水果和蔬菜。　(D) 葡萄牙。
   * Portugal (ˈportʃəgl) *n.* 葡萄牙

4. (**D**) "Feijoada" 是 ＿＿＿＿＿＿ 的一道風味非常獨特的菜。
   (A) 歐洲　　(B) 葡萄牙　　(C) 巴西　　(D) 里約熱內盧

5. (**B**) 巴西人通常 ＿＿＿＿＿＿ 吃 "feijoada" 這道菜。
   (A) 在假日　　(B) 在週末　　(C) 很匆忙地　　(D) 在海灘

TEST 18

Read the following passage, and choose the best answer for each question.

Recently in Greece many parents complained about the difficult homework which teachers gave to their children. The parents said most of the homework was a waste of time, and they wanted to stop it. Spain and Turkey are two countries which stopped homework recently. In Denmark, Germany and several other countries in Europe, teachers cannot set homework on weekends. In Holland, teachers allow pupils to stay at school to do their homework. The children are free to help one another. Similar arrangements also exist in some British schools.

Most parents agree that homework is unfair. A pupil who can do his homework in a quiet and comfortable room is in a much better position than a pupil who does his homework in a small, noisy room with the television on. Some parents help their children with their homework, while others don't.

1. Greek parents complained about _____
   (A) the strict teachers.
   (B) the unfair teachers.
   (C) too much homework.
   (D) the difficult homework.

2. In _____ , homework has been stopped.

   (A) Greece   (B) Turkey

   (C) Denmark   (D) Britain

3. In _____ , teachers can't set homework at weekends.

   (A) Greece   (B) Holland

   (C) Britain   (D) Germany

4. In Holland, _____

   (A) children can do homework at school.

   (B) children have to do homework without others' help.

   (C) children have less homework on weekends.

   (D) parents want to stop children's homework.

5. Most parents think homework unfair because _____

   (A) it is a waste of time.

   (B) all the children do their homework with the television on.

   (C) some parents help their children with their homework, but others don't.

   (D) some homework is easy, while some is difficult.

TEST 18 詳解

Recently in Greece many parents complained about the difficult homework *which teachers gave to their children*. The parents said most *of the homework* was a waste of time, *and* they wanted to stop it. Spain and Turkey are two countries *which stopped homework recently*.

最近在希臘，有很多父母抱怨，老師給孩子的家庭作業太難了。父母指出，大部份的家庭作業都是在浪費時間，所以他們想要阻止這件事。西班牙和土耳其這兩個國家，最近也廢除了家庭作業。

recently ('risṇtlɪ) *adv.* 最近　　Greece (gris) *n.* 希臘
complain (kəm'plen) *v.* 抱怨　　Spain (spen) *n.* 西班牙
Turkey ('tɝkɪ) *n.* 土耳其

In Denmark, Germany and several other countries in Europe, teachers cannot set homework *on weekends*. *In Holland,* teachers allow pupils to stay *at school to do their homework*. The children are free to help one another. Similar arrangements *also* exist *in some British schools*.

在丹麥、德國，和其他一些歐洲國家，老師週末時不可指派作業。在荷蘭，老師允許學生留校做作業，孩子可以自由地互相幫忙。在一些英國學校也有類似的安排。

Denmark ('dɛnmark) *n.* 丹麥　　Germany ('dʒɝmənɪ) *n.* 德國
set (sɛt) *v.* 指派　　Holland ('halənd) *n.* 荷蘭
pupil ('pjupḷ) *n.* 學生　　British ('brɪtɪʃ) *adj.* 英國的

Most parents agree *that* homework is unfair. A pupil *who can do his homework in a quiet and comfortable room* is in a *much* better position *than* a pupil *who does his homework in a small, noisy room with the television on.* Some parents help their children with their homework, *while* others don't.

　　許多父母都認為，家庭作業是不公平的。在安靜舒適的房間寫作業的學生，其處境，比在狹小、吵鬧，而且開著電視的房間寫作業的學生，要好很多。有些父母會協助孩子寫作業，而有些卻不會。

1. (**D**) 希臘的父母抱怨
　　(A) 老師太嚴格。　　　　　　(B) 老師不公平。
　　(C) 家庭作業太多。　　　　　　(D) 家庭作業太難。

2. (**B**) 在 ＿＿＿＿＿＿＿＿ ，家庭作業已經被廢除了。
　　(A) 希臘　　(B) 土耳其　　(C) 丹麥　　(D) 英國

3. (**D**) 在 ＿＿＿＿＿＿＿＿ ，老師在週末時不可以指派家庭作業。
　　(A) 希臘　　(B) 荷蘭　　(C) 英國　　(D) 德國

4. (**A**) 在荷蘭，
　　(A) 孩子可以在學校做家庭作業。
　　(B) 孩子做作業時不能有他人的協助。
　　(C) 孩子在週末時功課較少。
　　(D) 父母想要廢除孩子的家庭作業。

5. (**C**) 大多數父母認為，家庭作業是不公平的，因為
　　(A) 很浪費時間。
　　(B) 所有的孩子做功課時都開著電視。
　　(C) 有些父母會幫孩子做家庭作業，但有些不會。
　　(D) 有些家庭作業簡單，而有些很難。

TEST 19

Read the following passage, and choose the best answer for each question.

The native people of North America made general use of body painting. When warriors prepared for battle, they would paint themselves with bold designs. They concentrated on their faces which were decorated with red stripes, black masks or white circles around the eyes. These designs made the warrior look fierce and aggressive. Other peoples also used war paint. When the Romans invaded Britain, they found that the Ancient Britons painted themselves with blue paint called woad before going into battle.

Body painting can be used for occasions other than battles. The aboriginal peoples of Australia often decorate their bodies with bold white markings for a corroboree. It is a special meeting at which men dance and sing.

1. The best title for this article is _____
   (A) battle and body painting.
   (B) war paint.
   (C) body painting.
   (D) ways of body decoration.

2. There were _____ around the eyes of the native warriors of North America.

   (A) red stripes   (B) black masks

   (C) white circles   (D) blue woad

3. The bold designs focused on the _____ of the native warriors of North America.

   (A) bodies   (B) faces

   (C) arms and legs   (D) eyes

4. _____ wore "woad" for battle.

   (A) The Ancient Britons

   (B) The Romans

   (C) Australian aboriginal peoples

   (D) The native people of North America

5. A corroboree is a special occasion on which men

   _____

   (A) look fierce.   (B) must be bold.

   (C) dance and eat.   (D) sing and dance.

TEST 19 詳解

The native people *of North America* made general use *of body painting*. ***When** warriors prepared for battle*, they would paint themselves *with bold designs*. They concentrated on their faces ***which** were decorated with red stripes, black masks or white circles around the eyes*. These designs made the warrior look fierce and aggressive.

　　北美洲的土著通常會使用人體彩繪。當戰士準備要上戰場時,他們會在自己的身上,畫上十分醒目的圖案。他們比較著重臉部,會用紅色條紋、黑色面具,或在眼睛周圍塗上白色的圈圈來裝飾。這些圖案使得戰士看起來既凶猛,且具有攻擊性。

　　native〔'netɪv〕*adj.* 土著的　　***body painting*** 人體彩繪
　　warrior〔'wɔrɪə〕*n.* 戰士　　battle〔'bætḷ〕*n.* 戰役
　　bold〔bold〕*adj.* 醒目的;大膽的　　design〔dɪ'zaɪn〕*n.* 圖案
　　stripe〔straɪp〕*n.* 條紋　　fierce〔fɪrs〕*adj.* 凶猛的
　　aggressive〔ə'grɛsɪv〕*adj.* 具有攻擊性的

Other peoples *also* used war paint. ***When** the Romans invaded Britain*, they found ***that** the Ancient Britons painted themselves with blue paint called woad* before going into battle.

　　其他民族在出戰前也會在身上塗上顏料。當羅馬人侵略英國時,他們發現,古不列顛人,在上戰場前,會在身上塗一種叫靛藍的顏料。

　　people〔'pipḷ〕*n.* 民族　　***war paint*** 出戰前塗在臉上或身上的顏料
　　invade〔ɪn'ved〕*v.* 侵略　　Britain〔'brɪtṇ〕*n.* 英國
　　Briton〔'brɪtən〕*n.* 英國人;不列顛人(古代居住於大不列顛島南部的塞爾特人)
　　woad〔wod〕*n.* 靛藍(古代 Briton 人採集菘藍葉製成的染料,用以染身)

Body painting can be used *for occasions* *other than battles*.

The aboriginal peoples *of Australia often* decorate their bodies

with bold white markings *for a corroboree*. It is a special meeting

at **which** *men dance and sing.*

人體彩繪也可以用在戰爭以外的場合。澳洲的土著常會用醒目的白色花紋來裝飾身體，參加歌舞會。歌舞會是種大家一起唱歌跳舞的聚會。

occasion〔ə'keʒən〕*n.* 場合　　***other than*** 除了～之外
aboriginal〔ˌæbə'rɪdʒənḷ〕*adj.* 土著的　　marking〔'markɪŋ〕*n.* 花紋
corroboree〔kə'rɑbərɪ〕*n.* (澳洲土著為慶祝部落勝利等，於夜間舉行的) 歌舞會
meeting〔'mitɪŋ〕*n.* 聚會

1. (**C**) 本文最好的標題是
   (A) 戰爭與人體彩繪。　　(B) 出戰前塗在臉上或身上的顏料。
   (C) 人體彩繪。　　　　　(D) 裝飾身體的方式。

2. (**C**) 北美洲土著的戰士，其眼睛周圍會有
   (A) 紅色條紋。　　　　　(B) 黑色面具。
   (C) 白色圈圈。　　　　　(D) 藍色的靛藍。

3. (**B**) 北美洲土著的戰士，其醒目的圖案會集中在
   (A) 身體上。　　　　　　(B) 臉上。
   (C) 手臂和腿上。　　　　(D) 眼睛。
   * ***focus on*** 集中於

4. (**A**) ＿＿＿＿＿＿＿上戰場時會塗上靛藍。
   (A) 古不列顛人　　　　　(B) 羅馬人
   (C) 澳洲的土著　　　　　(D) 北美洲的土著

5. (**D**) 澳洲土著的歌舞會是種特殊的慶典，在慶典上人們
   (A) 看起來很凶猛。　　　(B) 必須要大膽。
   (C) 又跳舞又吃東西。　　(D) 又唱歌又跳舞。
   * occasion〔ə'keʒən〕*n.* 慶典

TEST 20

Refer to the following textbook index:

Assets	94-230
Dividends	83
Investment and taxation	314-316
Monopoly and antitrust	494
Strike	519
Unemployment and inflation	154-156

1. On which of the pages of the textbook would one look to find the cases of arbitration and mediation?
   (A) 83.   (B) 94.
   (C) 154.   (D) 519.

2. Which of the following pages would most likely contain a series of problems regarding exclusive control of a commodity or service?
   (A) 94-230.   (B) 154-156.
   (C) 494.   (D) 519.

3. On which of the pages would one find the information with regard to the stockholders of a company?
   (A) 83.   (B) 94-230.
   (C) 314-316.   (D) 494.

4. In which section of the index would one find information about a sharp and sudden rise of prices resulting from a too great expansion in paper money or bank credit?

(A) Assets.
(B) Investment and taxation.
(C) Monopoly and antitrust.
(D) Unemployment and inflation.

5. Under which heading would one find information on payments made by public corporations to its shareholders?

(A) Assets.
(B) Investment and taxation.
(C) Dividends.
(D) Monopoly and antitrust.

TEST 20 詳解

參考下列教科書索引：

資　　產 ……………………………………… 94-230
股　　息 ……………………………………… 83
投資和稅制 …………………………………… 314-316
壟斷和反托拉斯 ……………………………… 494
罷　　工 ……………………………………… 519
失業和通貨膨脹 ……………………………… 154-156

assets (ˋæsɛts) *n., pl.* 資產　　dividend (ˋdɪvəˏdɛnd) *n.* 股息
investment (ɪnˋvɛstmənt) *n.* 投資
taxation (tæksˋeʃən) *n.* 課稅；稅制　　monopoly (məˋnɑplɪ) *n.* 壟斷
antitrust (ˏæntɪˋtrʌst) *adj.* 反托拉斯的；反對獨占市場的
strike (straɪk) *n.* 罷工　　unemployment (ˏʌnɪmˋplɔɪmənt) *n.* 失業
inflation (ɪnˋfleʃən) *n.* 通貨膨脹

1. (**D**) 在這本教科書的哪一頁，可以找到仲裁和調停的例子？
   (A) 第 83 頁。　　　　　　　(B) 第 94 頁。
   (C) 第 154 頁。　　　　　　　(D) 第 519 頁。
   * arbitration (ˏɑrbəˋtreʃən) *n.* 仲裁；調停
     mediation (ˏmidɪˋeʃən) *n.* 仲裁；調停

2. (**C**) 下列哪一頁，最可能包含一連串有關商品或公共事業的獨占問題？
   (A) 第 94～230 頁。　　　　(B) 第 154～156 頁。
   (C) 第 494 頁。　　　　　　(D) 第 519 頁。
   * exclusive (ɪkˋsklusɪv) *adj.* 獨占的；排他的
     commodity (kəˋmɑdətɪ) *n.* 商品
     service (ˋsɝvɪs) *n.* 服務；公用事業

3. (**A**) 可以在哪一頁找到有關公司股東的資料？

(A) 第 83 頁。　　　　　(B) 第 94～230 頁。

(C) 第 314～316 頁。　　(D) 第 494 頁。

* ***with regard to*** 關於 (= *about*)
stockholder〔'stɑk,holdə〕*n.* 股東

4. (**D**) 可在索引的哪一部份，找到關於紙幣或銀行信用的擴張太大，而
造成價格遽升的資料？

(A) 資產。　　　　　　　(B) 投資和稅制。

(C) 壟斷和反托拉斯。　　(D) 失業和通貨膨脹。

* sharp〔ʃɑrp〕*adj.* 急劇的；猛烈的
expansion〔ɪk'spænʃən〕*n.* 擴張；擴大
credit〔'krɛdɪt〕*n.* 信用

5. (**C**) 在下列哪一個標題下的內文中，可找到公開招股公司支付其股東
多少錢的資料？

(A) 資產。　　　　　　　(B) 投資和稅制。

(C) 股息。　　　　　　　(D) 壟斷和反托拉斯。

* heading〔'hɛdɪŋ〕*n.* 標題
payment〔'pemənt〕*n.* 支付；付款
corporation〔,kɔrpə'reʃən〕*n.* 股份有限公司
public corporation 公開招股公司 (= *public company*)

TEST 21

Read the following passage, and choose the best answer for each question.

Traditional festivals are important events in the life of every Chinese, beginning right from childhood. Festivals such as Chinese New Year, the Dragon Boat Festival, the Mid-Autumn Festival, and the Winter Solstice are more or less evenly distributed across the four seasons. In China's traditional agricultural society, festivals served to mark the passing of time. Lifestyles of the people of the Republic of China today have undeniably changed a great deal since those times, and people now function according to a different concept of time, but the importance of traditional festivals in their lives has not faded.

1. Before the Chinese New Year, the last festival we Chinese here celebrate is _____
   (A) the Mid-Autumn Festival.
   (B) the Dragon Boat Festival.
   (C) the Winter Solstice.
   (D) the Ghost Festival.

2. With the passing of time, people's lifestyles in Taiwan have _____
   (A) remained the same.   (B) changed a lot.
   (C) changed little.   (D) appeared strange.

3. The importance of traditional festivals in the life of
   every Chinese can not be _____

   (A) seen.   (B) realized.
   (C) overemphasized.   (D) distributed.

4. We Chinese people eat mooncakes on _____

   (A) the Dragon Boat Festival.
   (B) the Mid-Autumn Festival.
   (C) the Winter Solstice.
   (D) the Lantern Festival.

5. Today, Taiwan's society has changed into _____

   (A) an industrial one.
   (B) an agricultural one.
   (C) an ancient one.
   (D) an eventful one.

TEST 21 詳解

Traditional festivals are important events *in the life of every Chinese, beginning right from childhood.* Festivals *such as Chinese New Year, the Dragon Boat Festival, the Mid-Autumn Festival, and the Winter Solstice* are *more or less evenly* distributed *across the four seasons.*

自孩提時代起，傳統節日在每個中國人的一生中，都是非常重要的事。像農曆新年、端午節、中秋節，和多至，這些節日幾乎是平均分布在四季之中。

traditional (trə'dɪʃənḷ) *adj.* 傳統的
festival ('fɛstəvḷ) *n.* 慶典；節日　　dragon ('dræɡən) *n.* 龍
Dragon Boat Festival 端午節
autumn ('ɔtəm) *n.* 秋天　　**Mid-Autumn Festival** 中秋節
solstice ('sɑlstɪs) *n.* 至；至日（指太陽距離赤道最遠時，一年有兩次。）
Winter Solstice 多至　　**more or less** 幾乎；或多或少
evenly ('ivənlɪ) *adv.* 平均地　　distribute (dɪ'strɪbjut) *v.* 分布

In China's traditional agricultural society, festivals served to mark the passing *of time.* Lifestyles *of the people of the Republic of China today* have *undeniably* changed *a great deal since those times,* **and** people *now* function *according to a different concept of time,* **but** the importance *of traditional festivals in their lives* has not faded.

在中國傳統農業社會中，節慶可以顯示時間的流逝。不可否認地，從那個時代起，中華民國人民的生活型態，已經大大地改變了。現代人的作息，是依照另一種不同的時間概念，不過，傳統節日在其日常生活中的重要性，並沒有消失。

> agricultural (ˌægrɪ'kʌltʃərəl) *adj.* 農業的　　serve (sɝv) *v.* 充當
> mark (mɑrk) *v.* 顯示　　undeniably (ˌʌndɪ'naɪəblɪ) *adv.* 不可否認地
> function ('fʌŋkʃən) *v.* 工作；活動
> concept ('kɑnsɛpt) *n.* 概念　　fade (fed) *v.* 逐漸消失

1. (**C**) 在農曆新年前，我們這裏的中國人，最後一個慶祝的節日爲
    (A) 中秋節。　　　　　　　　(B) 端午節。
    (C) 冬至。　　　　　　　　　(D) 鬼節。

2. (**B**) 隨著時間的流逝，台灣人民的生活型態
    (A) 仍維持不變。　　　　　　(B) 改變了很多。
    (C) 沒什麼改變。　　　　　　(D) 似乎變得很奇怪。

3. (**C**) 在每個中國人的生活中，傳統節日的重要性是
    (A) 不能被看見的。　　　　　(B) 不能被了解的。
    (C) 再怎麼強調也不爲過。　　(D) 不能被分配的。

    * *cannot be overemphasized* 再怎麼強調也不爲過

4. (**B**) 我們中國人在 ＿＿＿＿＿＿＿＿ 吃月餅。
    (A) 端午節　　　　　　　　　(B) 中秋節
    (C) 冬至　　　　　　　　　　(D) 元宵節

    * mooncake ('mun,kek) *n.* 月餅　　lantern ('læntən) *n.* 燈籠

5. (**A**) 現今的台灣社會已轉變爲
    (A) 工業社會。　　　　　　　(B) 農業社會。
    (C) 古代的社會。　　　　　　(D) 多事故的社會。

    * industrial (ɪn'dʌstrɪəl) *adj.* 工業的
      ancient ('enʃənt) *adj.* 古代的　　eventful (ɪ'vɛntfəl) *adj.* 多事故的

TEST 22

Read the following passage, and choose the best answer for each question.

The early adolescent seems to be in a state that is difficult for most adults to understand. Parents, in particular, are often at a loss for how to deal with someone they thought they knew but who now seems changed. Changeability and contradiction are characteristic of youngsters during this time. They want to be independent and reject parental control, appearing at times extremely rebellious. At the same time they conform almost sheepishly to their peers' standards of dress, music, and behavior. They seem to be completely self-centered and materialistic one moment, then suddenly shift to an altruistic giving of themselves in the service of some social or political cause. They can be extremely inconsiderate and tactless one day, remarkably sensitive the next. Their moods can change within minutes from being on top of the world to feeling that everything is hopeless. Consistency is totally missing, and these rapid shifts and contradictions seem hard to comprehend.

1. Parents find adolescents hard to understand because _____
   (A) they are always self-centered and inconsiderate.
   (B) they want to be independent.
   (C) the parents feel loss.
   (D) they are inconsistent.

2. The state of adolescence is _____
   (A) sheepish.   (B) consistent.
   (C) changeable.   (D) angry.

3. The author probably thinks _____
   (A) adolescence is a difficult period.
   (B) adolescents are bad.
   (C) adolescents are treated too softly in today's society.
   (D) parents should be more strict with their adolescent
       children.

4. Sometimes youngsters devote themselves to the service of
   some social or political cause because they are _____
   (A) altruistic.   (B) materialistic.
   (C) sensitive.   (D) tactless.

5. The author's tone in this passage is _____
   (A) contradictory.   (B) confused.
   (C) understanding.   (D) apologetic.

TEST 22 詳解

The early adolescent seems to be in a state *that is difficult for most adults to understand*. Parents, *in particular*, are *often* at a loss for *how* to deal with someone they thought they knew *but who now seems changed.*

剛進入青春期的青少年，似乎處在一個讓大多數成人難以理解的階段。尤其是父母，在面對一個他們原本認為是非常了解，可是現在似乎卻已經改變的人，通常會不知道該如何與他相處。

adolescent〔͵ædḷˈɛsṇt〕*n.* 青少年
state〔stet〕*n.* 狀態；階段　　adult〔əˈdʌlt〕*n.* 成人
at a loss 不知所措；困惑　　*deal with* 相處

Changeability and contradiction are characteristic of youngsters *during this time*. They want to be independent *and* reject parental control, *appearing at times extremely rebellious. At the same time* they conform *almost sheepishly* to their peers' standards *of dress, music, and behavior.*

這段時期的年輕人，特徵就是善變與矛盾。他們想要獨立，拒絕父母的控制，因此，有時會表現得非常叛逆。可是同時，他們卻會很怯懦地，遵從同儕對於服裝、音樂，以及行為的標準。

changeability (ˌtʃendʒə'bɪlətɪ) *n.* 善變
contradiction (ˌkɑntrə'dɪkʃən) *n.* 矛盾
be characteristic of 是～的特性
youngster ('jʌŋstɚ) *n.* 年輕人
reject (rɪ'dʒɛkt) *v.* 拒絕　　***at times*** 有時候 (= *sometimes*)
extremely (ɪk'strimlɪ) *adv.* 非常地
rebellious (rɪ'bɛljəs) *adj.* 叛逆的　　conform (ˈkən'fɔrm) *v.* 遵從
sheepishly ('ʃipɪʃlɪ) *adv.* 怯懦地　　peer (pɪr) *n.* 同儕

They seem to be *completely* self-centered and materialistic *one moment, then suddenly* shift to an altruistic giving *of themselves* in the service of *some social or political cause.*

有時，他們似乎是完全以自我爲中心，而且很現實，然後一下子，卻又變成十分樂於在一些社會及政治性的活動中，毫無保留地奉獻自己。

self-centered ('sɛlf'sɛntɚd) *adj.* 以自我爲中心的
materialistic (məˌtɪrɪəl'ɪstɪk) *adj.* 物質主義的；現實主義的
shift (ʃɪft) *v.* 轉變　　altruistic (ˌæltrʊ'ɪstɪk) *adj.* 利他的；無私的
cause (kɔz) *n.* 目標；理想

They can be *extremely* inconsiderate and tactless *one day, remarkably* sensitive *the next.* Their moods can change *within minutes from being on top of the world to feeling **that** everything is hopeless.* Consistency is *totally* missing, ***and*** these rapid shifts and contradictions seem hard to comprehend.

有時他們可以是非常不體貼而且不圓滑，可是隔天竟然出奇的敏感。他們的心情，可以在幾分鐘內，由非常高興，變成十分絕望。他們的言行，前後完全不一致，而這些快速的轉變和矛盾，似乎非常令人難以理解。

> inconsiderate〔͵ɪnkən'sɪdərɪt〕*adj.* 不體貼的
> tactless〔'tæktlɪs〕*adj.* 無機智的；不圓滑的
> remarkably〔rɪ'mɑrkəblɪ〕*adv.* 不尋常地
> sensitive〔'sɛnsətɪv〕*adj.* 敏感的
> ***on top of the world*** 高興極了
> consistency〔kən'sɪstənsɪ〕*n.*（言行）前後一致
> missing〔'mɪsɪŋ〕*adj.* 缺少的
> comprehend〔͵kɑmprɪ'hɛnd〕*v.* 理解

1. **(D)** 父母覺得青少年很難了解，是因為

   (A) 他們總是以自我為中心，而且不體貼。

   (B) 他們想要獨立。

   (C) 父母親有失落感。

   (D) <u>他們的言行前後不一致。</u>

   * inconsistent〔͵ɪnkən'sɪstənt〕*adj.*（言行）不一致的

2. **(C)** 青春期是一種 _____ 階段。

   (A) 怯懦的 　　　　　　　　(B) 前後一致的

   (C) <u>善變的</u> 　　　　　　　　(D) 生氣的

   * adolescence〔͵ædḷ'ɛsn̩s〕*n.* 青春期

3. **(A)** 作者可能認為

   (A) <u>青春期是一段困難的時期。</u>

   (B) 青少年都很壞。

   (C) 現今社會對待青少年的方式太溫和了。

   (D) 父母應該對青少年子女更嚴格。

4. (**A**) 有時候，年輕人會投身於一些社會及政治性的活動，是因爲
他們是

(A) 不自私的。　　　　　　(B) 現實的。

(C) 敏感的。　　　　　　　(D) 不圓滑的。

5. (**C**) 本文作者的語氣是

(A) 矛盾的。　　　　　　　(B) 困惑的。

(C) 能體諒的。　　　　　　(D) 抱歉的。

* tone〔ton〕*n.* 語氣
contradictory〔,kɑntrə'dıktərı〕*adj.* 矛盾的
understanding〔,ʌndɚ'stændıŋ〕*adj.* 能體諒的
apologetic〔ə,pɑlə'dʒɛtık〕*adj.* 抱歉的

閱讀測驗萬一考新聞英語，就可不必看文
章，以常識判斷，直接作答。

TEST 23

Read the following passage, and choose the best answer for each question.

The human race is only one small species of beings in the living world; many other groups exist among the creatures on this planet. However, human beings have a great influence on the rest of the world. People change the environment by building cities where forests once stood. People affect the water supply by using water for industry and agriculture. People affect weather conditions by increasing the amount of water in the air; when open land is changed into farms, the humidity of the atmosphere in that area increases because of the increased vegetation. Human beings change the air by adding pollutants like smoke from factories and fumes from automobile motors. Thus, it can be said that the human species changes the world through its actions and by its habits. People, in other words, are interfering with nature.

1. The main idea of this passage is to tell the reader that _____

   (A) human beings need to grow food.
   (B) human beings pollute the environment.
   (C) people's habits affect the world.
   (D) people should stop living in cities.

2. An increasing number of plants in a certain area will
   affect _____
   (A) people's activities.
   (B) the cultivation of land.
   (C) the development of industry and agriculture.
   (D) the humidity of the atmosphere.

3. On this planet, the Earth, live _____
   (A) only the human race.
   (B) only the wild animals.
   (C) a small species of beings.
   (D) all sorts of creatures.

4. The effect human actions and habits have on the rest
   of the world is _____
   (A) beneficial.   (B) healthy.
   (C) far-reaching.   (D) unknown.

5. Turning forests into building sites will _____
   (A) improve the quality of air.
   (B) change the face of the environment.
   (C) reduce the number of farms.
   (D) increase employment opportunities.

TEST 23 詳解

The human race is only one small species of beings *in the living world*; many other groups exist *among the creatures on this planet*. However, human beings have a great influence on the rest *of the world*.

在生物界中，人類只是一種渺小的生物；還有其他許多種類的生物生存在這個星球上。然而，人類對其他生物卻有很大的影響。

human race 人類 (= *human beings*)　species (ʹspiʃɪz) *n.* 種
being (ʹbiɪŋ) *n.* 生物　exist (ɪgʹzɪst) *v.* 存在
creature (ʹkritʃɚ) *n.* 生物　planet (ʹplænɪt) *n.* 行星
influence (ʹɪnfluəns) *n.* 影響

People change the environment *by building cities **where** forests once stood*. People affect the water supply *by using water for industry and agriculture*. People affect weather conditions *by increasing the amount of water in the air*; **when** *open land is changed into farms, the humidity of the atmosphere in that area* increases *because of the increased vegetation*. Human beings change the air *by adding pollutants like smoke from factories **and** fumes from automobile motors*.

人類在曾是森林的地方建造城市，因而改變了環境。人將水用於工業和農業，而影響了水的供給。人類增加空氣中的水分含量，因而影響了天氣狀況；當空地變成農田，該地區空氣中的濕度，會因植物增加而提高。人類使污染物增加，如工廠排放的煙，和汽車引擎的廢氣，進而改變了空氣。

stand〔stænd〕*v.* 位於;座落於　　humidity〔hju'mɪdətɪ〕*n.* 濕度
atmosphere〔'ætməs,fɪr〕*n.* 大氣;空氣
vegetation〔,vɛdʒə'teʃən〕*n.* 植物
add〔æd〕*v.* 增加　　pollutant〔pə'lutn̩t〕*n.* 污染物
fumes〔fjumz〕*n. pl.* 煙　　motor〔'motɚ〕*n.* 引擎

Thus, it can be said *that* the human species changes the world
through its actions *and* by its habits. People, *in other words*, are
interfering with nature.

因此,我們可以說,人類的行為和習慣,改變了世界。換句話說,人類正在干
擾大自然。

> *human species* 人類　　interfere〔,ɪntɚ'fɪr〕*v.* 干擾

1. (**C**) 本文的主旨是要告訴讀者,
   (A) 人類必須生產食物。　　　　(B) 人類污染了環境。
   (C) 人們的習慣影響了世界。　　(D) 人們不應該再住在城市。

2. (**D**) 當某地區的植物愈來愈多時,會影響
   (A) 人類的活動。　　　　　　　(B) 土地的耕種。
   (C) 工業和農業的發展。　　　　(D) 空氣中的濕度。
   * cultivation〔,kʌltə'veʃən〕*n.* 耕種

3. (**D**) 在地球這個星球上,
   (A) 只住著人類。　　　　　　　(B) 只有野生動物。
   (C) 住著一種渺小的生物。　　　(D) 住著各種生物。

4. (**C**) 人類的行為和習慣,對其餘生物的影響是
   (A) 有益的。　　(B) 健康的。　　(C) 深遠的。　　(D) 未知的。
   * far-reaching〔'far'ritʃɪŋ〕*adj.* 深遠的

5. (**B**) 將森林改變成建築用地,會
   (A) 改善空氣品質。　　　　　　(B) 改變環境的外觀。
   (C) 減少農田的數量。　　　　　(D) 增加就業機會。
   * site〔saɪt〕*n.* 用地;地點　　face〔fes〕*n.* 外觀

TEST 24

Read the following passage, and choose the best answer for each question.

Advertising is the difficult business of bringing information to great numbers of people. The purpose of an ad is to make people respond — to make them react to an idea, such as helping to prevent forest fires, or to make them want to buy a certain product or service.

At the beginning of the 20th century, advertising was described as "salesmanship in print." If this definition were expanded to include radio, television, and the Internet, it would still stand today. The most effective way to sell something is through person-to-person contact. But the cost is high. Because it takes a great deal of time, it increases the cost of the product or service. However, advertising distributes the selling message to many people at one time.

1. This article is mainly about _____
   (A) the definition of advertising.
   (B) advertising at the beginning of the 20th century.
   (C) why advertising is a difficult business.
   (D) the most effective way of selling a certain product.

2. According to this article, the most effective way to sell something is _____

(A) through advertising.

(B) through direct contact.

(C) through mail order.

(D) putting an ad on the Internet.

3. The cost of selling through advertising is _____ that of person-to-person selling.

(A) higher than　　　　(B) lower than

(C) the same as　　　　(D) not so low as

4. "Salesmanship in print" refers to selling by putting ads

_____

(A) on television.　　　(B) on the radio.

(C) in the newspaper.　(D) on the Internet.

5. From this article, we have learned that _____

(A) it is easy to make people buy something by advertising it.

(B) the purpose of an ad is only to make people buy a product or service.

(C) advertising brings the selling message to many people at one time, so it is more effective than person-to-person selling.

(D) the cost of person-to-person selling is high because it takes lots of time.

TEST 24 詳解

Advertising is the difficult business *of bringing information to great numbers of people*. The purpose *of an ad* is to make people respond — to make them react to an idea, *such as helping to prevent forest fires*, **or** to make them want to buy a certain product or service.

廣告是個不簡單的行業，它能提供資訊給許多人。廣告的目的，就是要使人們有反應 —— 讓人們對某種想法有回應，例如協助預防森林大火，或使人們想去購買某種產品或服務。

> advertising (ˈædvɚˌtaɪzɪŋ) *n.* 廣告 (業)　　**numbers of** 許多的
> ad (æd) *n.* 廣告 (= *advertisement* (ˌædvɚˈtaɪzmənt))
> respond (rɪˈspɑnd) *v.* 反應；回應　　react (rɪˈækt) *v.* 反應
> prevent (prɪˈvɛnt) *v.* 預防　　certain (ˈsɝtn̩) *adj.* 某種
> product (ˈprɑdʌkt) *n.* 產品

At the beginning of the 20th century, advertising was described as "salesmanship in print." *If this definition were expanded to include radio, television, and the Internet*, it would *still* stand *today*.

二十世紀初，廣告被形容爲「平面推銷術」。如果將此定義擴大，包括廣播、電視，和網際網路，這種定義在今日仍然是成立的。

> salesmanship (ˈselzmənˌʃɪp) *n.* 推銷術
> **in print** 以印刷的形式　　definition (ˌdɛfəˈnɪʃən) *n.* 定義
> expand (ɪkˈspænd) *v.* 擴大　　Internet (ˈɪntɚˌnɛt) *n.* 網際網路
> stand (stænd) *v.* 持續；有效

The *most* effective way *to sell something* is through person-to-person

contact. ***But*** the cost is high. ***Because*** *it takes a great deal of time,*

it increases the cost *of the product or service. However,* advertising

distributes the selling message *to many people at one time.*

賣東西最有效的方法，就是透過面對面的接觸。但是這種方式的成本很高，因為需要花費很多時間，所以會增加商品或服務的成本。然而，廣告能同時將銷售的訊息，散布給許多人知道。

effective (ə'fɛktɪv) *adj.* 有效的
person-to-person ('pɜsəntə'pɜsən) *adj.* 個人對個人的；直接的
distribute (dɪ'strɪbjut) *v.* 散布　　*at one time* 同時

1. (**A**) 本文主要是探討
　　(A) 廣告的定義。　　　　　　(B) 二十世紀初的廣告業。
　　(C) 爲何廣告是不簡單的行業。　(D) 銷售某個產品最有效的方法。

2. (**B**) 根據本文，賣東西最有效的方法就是
　　(A) 透過廣告。　　　　　　　(B) 透過直接的接觸。
　　(C) 透過郵購。　　　　　　　(D) 在網際網路上刊登廣告。
　　* *mail order* 郵購

3. (**B**) 透過廣告銷售東西的成本 ＿＿＿＿＿＿ 面對面銷售的成本。
　　(A) 高於　　　(B) 低於　　　(C) 等於　　　(D) 不會低於

4. (**C**) 「平面推銷術」是指經由在 ＿＿＿＿＿＿ 刊登廣告來銷售產品。
　　(A) 電視上　　(B) 廣播上　　(C) 報紙上　　(D) 網路上

5. (**D**) 由本文可知，
　　(A) 透過刊登廣告的方式，很容易使人們購買產品。
　　(B) 廣告的目的，只是要使人們去購買某種產品或服務。
　　(C) 廣告可以同時將銷售的訊息散布給很多人知道，所以它比面對面的銷售方式更有效。
　　(D) 面對面銷售的成本很高，因爲要花很多時間。

TEST 25

Read the following passage, and choose the best answer for each question.

MARKHAM PLUMBING & HEATING
Since 1935
Plumbing and Heating Installation
LARGE OR SMALL REPAIRS
RESIDENTIAL · COMMERCIAL
FREE ESTIMATES
N. J. State License # 4807
24 Hour 7 Day Service

228 - 4495

461 GORDON WAY
HARRINGTON

---

1. What service is offered free by Markham Plumbing & Heating?

   (A) Installation.　　　　　(B) State licensing.
   (C) Cost estimates.　　　　(D) Large or small repairs.

2. In the ad, which of the following indicates that Markham Plumbing & Heating has been in business for a long time?
   (A) "Since 1935"
   (B) "N.J. State License # 4807"
   (C) "24 Hour 7 Day Service"
   (D) "Plumbing and Heating Installation"

3. For which of the following problems would one call Markham Plumbing & Heating?

   (A) A leak in the roof.

   (B) A gas leak in the refrigerator.

   (C) A short circuit in a wall plug that causes all the lights to go out.

   (D) A broken bathroom pipe that is leaking water all over the floor.

4. The words "Residential · Commercial" in the ad indicate that Markham Plumbing & Heating

   (A) is licensed as a commercial establishment to do work for private residences.

   (B) is a profit-making business with a plumber always in residence.

   (C) operates from a private home but makes commercial repairs.

   (D) does work for private homes as well as for business.

5. What information certifies the company in the State of N.J.?

   (A) "24 Hour 7 Day Service"

   (B) "License # 4807"

   (C) "Since 1935"

   (D) "228-4495"

TEST 25 詳解

馬可漢水管暖氣工程公司

1935 年創立

水管和暖氣裝設

大小工程修理

住家公司免費估價

紐澤西州執照號碼：4807

全週每日 24 小時服務

電話：228-4495

哈靈頓市高登道 461 號

---

plumbing（ˋplʌmɪŋ）*n.* 水管裝設   heating（ˋhitɪŋ）*n.* 暖氣設備
installation（͵ɪnstəˋleʃən）*n.* 安裝
residential（͵rɛzəˋdɛnʃəl）*adj.* 住家的
commercial（kəˋmɝʃəl）*adj.* 商業的；營利的
estimate（ˋɛstəmɪt）*n.* 估價

1. (**C**) 「馬可漢水管暖氣工程公司」免費提供什麼服務？
   (A) 裝設。 (B) 州照登記。
   (C) <u>估價。</u> (D) 大小工程修理。

2. (**A**) 在這則廣告中，下列何者指出，「馬可漢水管暖氣工程公司」已經經營很久了？
   (A) 「<u>1935 年創設</u>」
   (B) 「紐澤西州執照號碼：4807」
   (C) 「全週每日 24 小服務」
   (D) 「水管和暖氣裝設」

   * ad（æd）*n.* 廣告（= *advertisement*）

3. (**D**)　如果有下列哪一項問題，可以通知「馬可漢水管暖氣工程公司」？

(A) 屋頂漏水。

(B) 冰箱漏氣。

(C) 牆上插頭發生短路，使得所有電燈熄滅。

(D) 浴室水管破裂，水漏得滿地都是。

　* leak〔lik〕*n.,v.* 漏　　circuit〔'sʒkɪt〕*n.* 電路

　　plug〔plʌg〕*n.* 插頭　　***go out*** 熄滅

　　pipe〔paɪp〕*n.* 水管

4. (**D**)　在廣告中，"Residential‧Commercial"這兩個字是指，「馬可漢水管暖氣工程公司」是

(A) 登記許可的商業機構，可承包住家工程。

(B) 隨時有修水管工人駐任的營利事業。

(C) 私家經營，但是可承包商業機構的修理工程。

(D) 可包辦住家和公司工程。

　* licensed〔'laɪsn̩st〕*adj.* 有執照的

　　establishment〔ə'stæblɪʃmənt〕*n.* 公司；機構

　　residence〔'rɛzədəns〕*n.* 住宅　　profit〔'prɑfɪt〕*n.* 利益

　　plumber〔'plʌmɚ〕*n.* 水管工人　　operate〔'ɑpə,ret〕*v.* 經營

5. (**B**)　下列何者證明，在紐澤西州的這家公司領有執照？

(A) 「全週每日 24 小時服務」

(B) 「執照號碼：4807」

(C) 「1935 年創立」

(D) 「電話：228-4495」

　* certify〔'sʒtə,faɪ〕*v.* 證明～合格；發執照給～

TEST 26

Read the following passage, and choose the best answer for each question.

The Yangtze River is not the longest, the widest, or the mightiest river in the world. But in one sense, it is the most important river, because it serves more people than any other. In every way the Yangtze is China's life stream.

The Yangtze isn't just a trade river, along which goods are picked up and distributed. It is an agricultural river, too. Networks of irrigation ditches stretch out from it to millions of farms. There people work endlessly, raising their family's food and the nation's food.

The Yangtze River begins somewhere high in northern Tibet, hurtling down from a three-mile height. It surges for hundreds of miles, roars through canyons, and picks up branches. Only in the last 1,000 miles of its 3,200-mile journey does the Yangtze become China's blessing.

1. The Yangtze River begins its journey somewhere in
   the _____ part of Tibet.
   (A) central   (B) south
   (C) north   (D) eastern

2. How many miles does the river travel?

   (A) One thousand miles.

   (B) Thirty-two hundred miles.

   (C) Thirty-two thousand miles.

   (D) Hundreds of miles.

3. The upper part of the Yangtze River _____

   (A) flows through wide plains.

   (B) rushes down from high mountains.

   (C) is good for navigation.

   (D) is more valuable than the lower part.

4. The Yangtze River is _____

   (A) primarily a trade river.

   (B) not only a trade but an agricultural river.

   (C) a famous river mainly because it surges for hundreds of miles.

   (D) not the longest river in the world, but the widest and mightiest one.

5. From this article we have learned that _____

   (A) millions of farms along the river are often flooded.

   (B) a dam should be built to hold back the waters in the upper part of the river.

   (C) the nation's food depends only on the Yangtze River.

   (D) The Yangtze River is China's source of strength.

TEST 26 詳解

The Yangtze River is not the longest, the widest, *or* the mightiest river *in the world*. *But in one sense*, it is the *most* important river, *because it serves more people than any other*. *In every way* the Yangtze is China's life stream.

長江並不是世界上最長、最寬，或是最大的河。可是就某方面而言，它卻是最重要的河，因為使用長江的人，比使用其他河川的人多。長江在各方面，都可算是中國的生命之河。

> mighty ('maɪtɪ) *adj.* 巨大的　　*in one sense* 就某方面而言
> serve (sɜv) *v.* 供～使用　　stream (strim) *n.* 小河

The Yangtze isn't *just* a trade river, *along which goods are picked up and distributed*. It is an agricultural river, *too*. Networks *of irrigation ditches* stretch out *from it to millions of farms*. *There* people work *endlessly, raising their family's food and the nation's food*.

長江不只是一條裝載貨物，和分配貨物的運河。它也是一條農業用河。灌溉渠道的網路，從長江延伸至上百萬個農田。在那裏人們不停地工作，種植家庭和國家所需的食物。

> goods (gʊdz) *n.pl.* 貨物　　*pick up* 裝載
> network ('nɛt,wɜk) *n.* 網狀組織　　irrigation (,ɪrə'geʃən) *n.* 灌溉
> ditch (dɪtʃ) *n.* 溝渠　　stretch (strɛtʃ) *v.* 延伸　　raise (rez) *v.* 種植

The Yangtze River begins *somewhere high in northern Tibet, hurtling down from a three-mile height*. It surges *for hundreds of miles*, roars *through canyons*, *and* picks up branches.

Only in the last 1,000 miles of its 3,200-mile journey does the

Yangtze become China's blessing.

　　長江起源於西藏北部的某高地，從三英哩高的地方奔馳而下。河水洶湧綿延了好幾百英哩，從峽谷間呼嘯而過，沿途匯集了許多支流。在長江三千兩百英哩的旅程中，只有最後一千英哩成爲中國人的福祉。

Tibet〔tɪ'bɛt〕*n.* 西藏　　　hurtle〔'hɝtḷ〕*v.* 奔馳
surge〔sɝdʒ〕*v.* 洶湧　　　roar〔ror〕*v.*（海、風浪等）怒號；呼嘯
canyon〔'kænjən〕*n.* 峽谷　***pick up*** 收集　　branch〔bræntʃ〕*n.* 支流

1.(**C**)　長江起源於西藏 ＿＿＿＿＿＿ 的某處。
　　(A) 中部　　　(B) 南部　　　(C) 北部　　　(D) 東部

2.(**B**)　長江流經幾英哩？
　　(A) 一千英哩。　　　　　　　(B) 三千兩百英哩。
　　(C) 三萬兩千英哩。　　　　　(D) 幾百英哩。

3.(**B**)　長江上游
　　(A) 流經寬廣的平原。　　　　(B) 從高山奔馳而下。
　　(C) 利於航行。　　　　　　　(D) 比下游更有價值。
　　* plain〔plen〕*n.* 平原　　navigation〔ˌnævə'geʃən〕*n.* 航行

4.(**B**)　長江
　　(A) 是主要供貿易往來的河。
　　(B) 不但可供貿易往來，而且是農業用河。
　　(C) 是一條有名的河流，因爲它洶湧綿延好幾百英哩。
　　(D) 不是世界上最長的河，但卻是最寬、最大的河。
　　* primarily〔'praɪˌmɛrəlɪ〕*adv.* 主要地

5.(**D**)　從本文我們可知，
　　(A) 長江沿岸有好幾百萬個農田常被淹沒。
　　(B) 應該建造一座水壩，來抑制河川上游的水。
　　(C) 全國食物完全依賴長江。　(D) 長江是中國力量的泉源。
　　* flood〔flʌd〕*v.* 氾濫；淹沒　　dam〔dæm〕*n.* 水壩
　　hold back 抑制

TEST 27

Read the following passage, and choose the best answer for each question.

The hamburger is one of the most popular foods in the country. Americans eat about forty billion of them a year.

Charles Kuralt, of CBS-TV News, started keeping an <u>account</u> of the various names for the different kinds and sizes of burgers around the country. He found king burgers, queen burgers, mini burgers, maxi burgers, tuna burgers, poppa burgers, momma burgers, and baby burgers. In the South, he ate Dixie burgers, and in Washington, D.C., he ate Capitol burgers. Some restaurant owners named burgers after themselves: Buddy burgers, Cluck burgers, Juan burgers, and dozens more.

No matter what they're called, Americans eat a lot of them!

1. The best title is _____
    (A) A Man Who Loves Hamburgers.
    (B) Many Kinds of Burgers.
    (C) American Foods.
    (D) Eating in America.

2. In the South, Charles ate _____
    (A) Capitol burgers.　　　(B) poppa burgers.
    (C) Dixie burgers.　　　(D) Buddy burgers.

3. Americans eat about forty billion hamburgers each _____

    (A) year.   (B) week.

    (C) day.   (D) month.

4. One kind of burger not mentioned in the story is the _____

    (A) tuna burger.   (B) Jake burger.

    (C) maxi burger.   (D) Dixie burger.

5. The underlined word "account" means _____

    (A) recipe.   (B) record.

    (C) diary.   (D) column.

TEST 27 詳解

The hamburger is one *of the most popular foods* in the country. Americans eat about forty billion of them *a year*.

漢堡是這個國家最受歡迎的食物之一。每年,美國人會吃大約四百億個漢堡。

> hamburger〔'hæmbɝɡɚ〕*n.* 漢堡 (= *burger*)
> billion〔'bɪljən〕*n.* 十億

Charles Kuralt, *of CBS-TV News*, started keeping an <u>account</u> of the various names *for the different kinds and sizes of burgers around the country*. He found king burgers, queen burgers, mini burgers, maxi burgers, tuna burgers, poppa burgers, momma burgers, and baby burgers. *In the South*, he ate Dixie burgers, *and in Washington, D.C.*, he ate Capitol burgers. Some restaurant owners named burgers *after themselves*: Buddy burgers, Cluck burgers, Juan burgers, and dozens more.

哥倫比亞廣播公司新聞部的查爾斯・庫拉特,記錄了全國不同種類和大小的漢堡名稱。他發現有國王漢堡、皇后漢堡、迷你漢堡、超大漢堡、鮪魚漢堡、爸爸漢堡、媽媽漢堡,和嬰兒漢堡。在南方,他吃到南方漢堡,而在首都華盛頓,他吃到國會漢堡。有些餐廳老板會用自己的名字為漢堡命名:巴蒂漢堡、克拉克漢堡、瓊漢堡,還有許多其他名稱的漢堡。

CBS 哥倫比亞廣播公司 (= *Columbia Broadcasting System*)
account〔ə'kaʊnt〕*n.* 記錄　　tuna〔'tunə〕*n.* 鮪魚
Dixie〔'dɪksɪ〕*n.* 美國南部各州別稱
Washington D.C. （美國首都）華盛頓；哥倫比亞特區
（ = *District of Columbia* ）
Capitol〔'kæpətḷ〕*n.* 美國國會大廈　　*name…after~* 以~命名…
dozen〔'dʌzn̩〕*n.* 一打　　*dozens of* 幾十個；很多個

No matter what they're called, Americans eat a lot of them!
不管漢堡叫什麼名字，美國人都吃很多！

1. (**B**) 本文最好的標題是
　　(A) 一個喜愛漢堡的人。　　(B) 許多種類的漢堡。
　　(C) 美國食物。　　　　　　(D) 美國飲食。

2. (**C**) 查爾斯在南方吃到了
　　(A) 國會漢堡。　　　　　　(B) 爸爸漢堡。
　　(C) 南方漢堡。　　　　　　(D) 巴蒂漢堡。

3. (**A**) 美國人每 ＿＿＿＿＿＿＿ 吃了約四百億個漢堡。
　　(A) 年　　　　(B) 星期　　　　(C) 天　　　　(D) 月

4. (**B**) 本文沒提到的漢堡是
　　(A) 鮪魚漢堡。　　　　　　(B) 傑克漢堡。
　　(C) 超大漢堡。　　　　　　(D) 南方漢堡。

5. (**B**) 劃底線的字 "account"，意思是
　　(A) 食譜。　　(B) 記錄。　　(C) 日記。　　(D) 專欄。
　　* recipe〔'rɛsəpɪ〕*n.* 食譜　　diary〔'daɪərɪ〕*n.* 日記
　　column〔'kɑləm〕*n.* 專欄

TEST 28

Read the following passage, and choose the best answer for each question.

Basketball is one sport — perhaps the only sport — whose exact origin can safely be stated. During the winter of 1891-1892, Dr. James Naismith, a college instructor in Springfield, Massachusetts, invented the game of basketball in order to provide exercise for the students between the closing of the football season and the opening of the baseball season. He attached fruit baskets overhead on the walls at two ends of the gymnasium, and, using a soccer ball, organized nine-man teams to play his new game in which the purpose was to toss the ball into one basket and to keep the opposing team from tossing the ball into the other basket. Although there have since been many changes in the rules, the game is basically the same today.

1. When was basketball invented?
   (A) Earlier than football.
   (B) Later than football.
   (C) At the same time as football.
   (D) The exact origin was not known.

2. How many members were there on the first basketball team?
   (A) Five.   (B) Nine.
   (C) Ten.   (D) Indefinite.

3. Basketball was invented because _____

    (A) students needed winter exercise.

    (B) students were tired of playing football and baseball.

    (C) it could be played indoors.

    (D) Dr. Naismith thought it was more fun than other games.

4. Where was the first basketball game played?

    (A) On a university football field.

    (B) On a farm.

    (C) In a gym.

    (D) In Dr. Naismith's yard.

5. What equipment was used in the first basketball game?

    (A) Fruit baskets and a soccer ball.

    (B) A basketball and a gymnasium.

    (C) A gymnasium and fruit baskets.

    (D) No special equipment was used.

TEST 28 詳解

Basketball is one sport — *perhaps the only sport* — **whose exact origin can safely be stated.** *During the winter of 1891-1892,* Dr. James Naismith, *a college instructor in Springfield, Massachusetts,* invented the game *of basketball* **in order to provide exercise for the students** *between the closing of the football season* **and the opening of the baseball season.**

籃球是一種——也許是唯一的一種——可以確切地說出起源的運動。在一八九一到一八九二年的冬天，詹姆斯·奈史密斯博士，他是麻塞諸塞州春田市的一位大學講師，為了讓學生在橄欖球季結束後，到棒球季開始前這段期間，仍可以做些運動，而發明了籃球比賽。

> safely (ˋseflɪ) *adv.* 確實地　　origin (ˋɔrədʒɪn) *n.* 起源
> instructor (ɪnˋstrʌktə) *n.* 大學講師
> football (ˋfʊt͵bɔl) *n.* 橄欖球；美式足球

He attached fruit baskets *overhead on the walls at two ends of the gymnasium,* **and,** *using a soccer ball,* organized nine-man teams to play his new game **in which the purpose was to toss the ball into one basket and to keep the opposing team from tossing the *ball into the other basket.* ***Although*** *there have since been many*

changes in the rules, the game is *basically* the same *today*.

他把裝水果的籃子，高高地綁在體育館兩端的牆壁上，用足球來投球。他組織了兩支九人的球隊，來玩這個新的運動。這個運動的目標，是要把球投進一個籃框裡，並且防止敵隊把球投進另一個籃框。雖然從那時起，籃球的規則已經改變很多，但現在這個運動基本上還是一樣的。

> attach〔əˋtætʃ〕v. 綁；繫　　overhead〔ˏovɚˋhɛd〕adv. 在高處
> gymnasium〔dʒɪmˋnezɪəm〕n. 體育館（= gym）　soccer〔ˋsɑkɚ〕n. 足球
> toss〔tɔs〕v. 投擲　　opposing〔əˋpozɪŋ〕adj. 敵對的

1. (**B**) 籃球是何時發明的？

    (A) 比橄欖球早。　　　　　　(B) <u>比橄欖球晚。</u>

    (C) 和橄欖球同時。　　　　　(D) 正確的起源並不清楚。

2. (**B**) 第一支籃球隊有幾個人？

    (A) 五人。　　(B) <u>九人。</u>　　(C) 十人。　　(D) 不確定。

    * indefinite〔ɪnˋdɛfənɪt〕adj. 不確定的

3. (**A**) 發明籃球是因爲

    (A) <u>學生需要冬季運動。</u>

    (B) 學生們厭煩了打橄欖球和棒球。

    (C) 它可以在室內打。

    (D) 奈史密斯博士覺得籃球比其他運動有趣。

4. (**C**) 第一場籃球賽在哪裏舉行？

    (A) 在大學橄欖球場。　　　　(B) 在農場上。

    (C) <u>在體育館裏。</u>　　　　　　(D) 在奈史密斯博士的庭院裏。

5. (**A**) 在第一場的籃球賽使用了哪些裝備？

    (A) <u>水果籃和足球。</u>　　　　(B) 籃球和體育館。

    (C) 體育館和水果籃。　　　　(D) 並未使用任何特殊的裝備。

TEST 29

Read the following passage, and choose the best answer for each question.

The children were working hard at their desks when a big truck stopped outside the village school. Two smiling young women and one man got out of the truck. The children knew one of the women. She lived in the village, and sometimes came to school to examine them for signs of illness. The man carried something in his hand called a spray gun. The children knew what it was and knew what to do. Quickly they ran outside, lined up and knelt on the ground before the man. Some thought it was great fun and laughed and shouted. Some were afraid and cried. But everyone got well dusted with spray powder before the truck moved on. In other villages, there were other trucks stopping at one house after another. The walls in every house were sprayed.

1. Why did the people in that village take the spray?
   (A) for fun
   (B) to kill insects
   (C) to prevent disease
   (D) to protect the people in the truck

2. How many people came to the village to spray the inhabitants?
   (A) 1   (B) 2   (C) 3   (D) 4

3. Which of the following statements is true?

   (A) The children had never been treated this way before.

   (B) The children had been sprayed many times and knew it would be painful.

   (C) The children had never been sprayed before, so many of them were scared.

   (D) The children had been sprayed before, and some of them liked it.

4. Which of the following describes the people in the truck?

   (A) They were threatening.

   (B) They were friendly.

   (C) They were attractive.

   (D) They were unhealthy.

5. What did the children do when they saw the truck?

   (A) They took their medicine.

   (B) They knelt under their desks.

   (C) They ran out of the classroom.

   (D) They showed respect to the man because he was a great doctor.

TEST 29 詳解

The children were working *hard at their desks* **when** a big truck stopped *outside the village school*. Two smiling young women **and** one man got out of the truck.

當一輛大卡車停在村子那所學校的外面時，孩子們正在書桌前用功。有兩個面帶微笑的年輕女子，和一個男人從卡車上下來。

The children knew one *of the women*. She lived *in the village*, **and** sometimes came to school *to examine them for signs of illness*. The man carried something *in his hand called a spray gun*. The children knew **what** *it was* **and** knew **what** *to do*. *Quickly* they ran *outside*, lined up **and** knelt *on the ground before the man*.

孩子們認識其中一位女子。她住在村子裡，有時候會來學校，檢查學童們是否有生病的症狀。那個男人手上，拿著一種叫做噴霧槍的東西。學童們知道它是什麼，也知道自己該做些什麼。他們迅速地跑到外面，排成一排，跪在男人面前。

examine〔ɪgˈzæmɪn〕v. 檢查　　sign〔saɪn〕n. 徵兆；症狀
spray〔spre〕n. 噴霧　v. 噴灑　　***line up*** 排隊　　kneel〔nil〕v. 跪

Some thought *it was great fun* **and** laughed and shouted. Some were afraid and cried. **But** everyone got *well* dusted *with spray* *powder **before** the truck moved on. In other villages, there were other trucks stopping at one house after another. The walls in every house were sprayed.*

有些孩童覺得很好玩，一邊笑，一邊叫。有些則害怕得哭了。但在卡車**離開**之前，每個孩童身上都有噴灑了一層粉末。在其他村莊，也有別的卡車**挨家挨戶**地停靠著。每一戶人家的牆壁都被噴灑上一層粉末。

dust〔dʌst〕v. 噴灑　　powder〔ˈpaʊdə〕n. 粉末

1. (**C**) 爲什麼那村莊的人要接受粉末的噴灑？
   (A) 爲了好玩
   (B) 爲了除蟲
   (C) 爲了預防疾病
   (D) 爲了保護卡車上的人

2. (**C**) 有多少人到這村裏向居民噴灑粉末？
   (A) 一個　　(B) 二個　　(C) 三個　　(D) 四個
   * inhabitant〔ɪnˈhæbətənt〕n. 居民

3. (**D**) 下列敘述何者爲眞？
   (A) 孩子們以前不曾被這樣對待過。
   (B) 孩子們已經被噴灑了好幾次，而且知道這會很痛。
   (C) 孩子們從來不曾被噴灑過，所以他們之中有很多人都很害怕。
   (D) 孩子們曾經被噴灑過，其中有些人還蠻喜歡的。

4. (**B**) 下列對卡車上的人的描述，何者正確？
   (A) 他們具有威脅性。
   (B) 他們是友善的。
   (C) 他們很吸引人。
   (D) 他們是不健康的。

5. (**C**) 當孩子們看到卡車時，他們有什麼反應？
   (A) 他們吃藥。
   (B) 他們跪在書桌底下。
   (C) 他們衝出教室。
   (D) 他們非常尊敬那男人，因爲他是個偉大的醫生。

TEST 30

Read the following passage, and choose the best answer for each question.

Instructions for the Use of Your New Hercules Vacuum Cleaner

1. Do not oil. The motors are permanently lubricated.

2. Do not operate cleaner without dust bag.

3. Disconnect power cord from electrical outlet before changing bags.

4. Do not run cleaner over power cord.

5. Avoid picking up hard objects with your cleaner to prevent bag breakage, hose clogging, or motor damage.

6. Warning: Electric shock could occur if used outdoors or on wet surfaces.

1. According to the directions, where or when is it dangerous to use this cleaner?

   (A) Outdoors.
   (B) Indoors.
   (C) When it is disconnected.
   (D) When it has not been lubricated.

2. Using this cleaner on a wet surface may cause

   (A) the hose to clog.
   (B) the bag to break.
   (C) electric shock.
   (D) oil leakage.

3. Which of the following will NOT damage the cleaner?

   (A) Picking up nails with it.
   (B) Clogging the hose.
   (C) Running over its power cord.
   (D) Using a dust bag.

4. How often should you oil the cleaner?

   (A) Once every use.
   (B) Once every three months.
   (C) Once a year.
   (D) Never.

5. What should you not use your vacuum cleaner to clean?

   (A) Hair.   (B) Soil.
   (C) Coins.   (D) Dust.

TEST 30 詳解

新赫克力斯真空吸塵器使用說明

1. 不要上油。馬達可永保潤滑。
2. 無儲塵袋時，不可操作吸塵器。
3. 更換儲塵袋時，務必將電源線自插座上取下。
4. 不要使吸塵器壓到電線。
5. 避免用吸塵器吸取硬物，以免儲塵袋破裂、軟管阻塞，或馬達受損。
6. 注意：在戶外或潮溼表面上使用吸塵器會遭電擊。

---

instructions (ɪnˈstrʌkʃənz) *n. pl.* 指示；使用說明
Hercules (ˈhɝkjəˌliz) *n.* 赫克力斯 (希臘神話中的大力士)
vacuum (ˈvækjuəm) *n.* 真空　　cleaner (ˈklinɚ) *n.* 吸塵器
vacuum cleaner 真空吸塵器　　oil (ɔɪl) *v.* 上油
lubricate (ˈlubrɪˌket) *v.* 使潤滑
disconnect (ˌdɪskəˈnɛkt) *v.* 使分離
outlet (ˈautˌlɛt) *n.* 插座　　***run over*** 輾過
power cord 電線　　***pick up*** 收集；吸取
breakage (ˈbrekɪdʒ) *n.* 破裂　　hose (hoz) *n.* 軟管
clog (klɑg , klɔg) *v.* 阻塞　　shock (ʃɑk) *n.* 電擊

1. (**A**) 根據使用說明，在何時何地使用吸塵器是危險的？
   (A) 戶外。　　　　　　　　 (B) 室內。
   (C) 不接電源時。　　　　　 (D) 不加潤滑油時。

2. (**C**) 在潮濕表面上使用吸塵器，可能導致
   (A) 軟管阻塞。　　　　　　 (B) 儲塵袋破裂。
   (C) 電擊。　　　　　　　　 (D) 漏油。

3.(**D**) 下列何種情況不會損害吸塵器？

    (A) 用吸塵器吸鐵釘。   (B) 軟管阻塞。

    (C) 壓到吸塵器的電線。   (D) <u>使用儲塵袋。</u>

4.(**D**) 你該多久替吸塵器上一次油？

    (A) 每使用一次就上一次油。   (B) 每三個月一次。

    (C) 每年一次。   (D) <u>不需要。</u>

5.(**C**) 你不該用吸塵器吸下列何者？

    (A) 頭髮。   (B) 土壤。

    (C) <u>硬幣。</u>   (D) 灰塵。

《強迫得分祕訣》

    在大規模的考試中，英文教授出題，常常不知不覺會平均分配答案，如：

1. (A)
2. (B)
3. (?)
4. (C)
5. (C)

> 第3題不會，選什麼？第3題選(D)，答對的可能性最大。
> 選答案(C)，答對的機會最小，答案(B)的機會也小。

    同學用「刪除法」，把絕對不可能的答案刪掉，再用這種方法，閱讀測驗就容易得滿分了。注意：如果一個大題，平均分配答案，則其他大題也可能一樣，反之亦然。

TEST 31

Read the following passage, and choose the best answer for each question.

Did you know that a change in the weather can affect your behavior? For example, a Japanese scientist studied the number of packages and umbrellas left behind on buses and streetcars in Tokyo. He found that passengers were most forgetful on days when the barometer fell. Also, after studying patterns of car accidents in Ontario, the Canadians found that most accidents took place when the barometer fell. Other studies show that a sudden rise in temperature within a low-pressure area can lead to destructive acts, including suicide.

1. According to this passage, a change in the weather _____
   (A) is caused by the behavior of people.
   (B) affects the way people behave.
   (C) affects personal behavior only in Tokyo.
   (D) affects only those who ride buses and streetcars.

2. When the barometer fell in Tokyo _____
   (A) hundreds of people were injured by the falling debris.
   (B) people's memories improved.
   (C) people always brought umbrellas with them when they went out.
   (D) people tended to forget things on public transportation.

3. The studies mentioned in this passage show that changes in the weather produce all but which of the following?

   (A) temporary forgetfulness
   (B) a lack of coordination in car drivers
   (C) a reduction of pressure at work
   (D) suicides

4. It can be inferred that when the barometer rises _____

   (A) more people will commit suicide.
   (B) people will be able to concentrate better.
   (C) people will suffer less pressure.
   (D) people will not drive as much.

5. What is Ontario?

   (A) It is a research institute.
   (B) It is a barometer.
   (C) It is a city.
   (D) It is a Canadian province.

TEST 31 詳解

Did you know ***that*** *a change in the weather can affect your*

behavior? *For example*, a Japanese scientist studied the number

of packages and umbrellas left behind on buses and streetcars in

Tokyo. He found ***that*** *passengers were most forgetful on days **when***

***the barometer fell**.*

你知道天氣的改變會影響你的行爲嗎？舉例來說，有位日本科學家曾研究過，遺留在東京的巴士和電車上的包裹及雨傘的數目，結果發現，當氣壓降低時，旅客最健忘。

package (ˈpækɪdʒ) *n.* 包裹　　***leave~behind*** 遺留~
streetcar (ˈstritˌkɑr) *n.* 電車　　forgetful (fəˈgɛtfəl) *adj.* 健忘的
barometer (bəˈrɑmətɚ) *n.* 氣壓計　　fall (fɔl) *v.* 下降

Also, ***after*** *studying patterns of car accidents in Ontario*, *the*

*Canadians found **that** most accidents took place **when** the barometer*

fell. Other studies show ***that*** *a sudden rise in temperature **within a***

low-pressure area can lead to destructive acts, including suicide.

同樣地，在加拿大安大略省，也研究過當地車禍發生的模式，結果發現，大部份的車禍也都發生在氣壓下降時。其他研究也顯示，在低壓地區，如果氣溫驟升，會導致破壞性行爲，自殺也包括在內。

also (ˈɔlso) *adv.* 同樣地　　pattern (ˈpætən) *n.* 型態；模式
Ontario (ɑnˈtɛrɪˌo) *n.* 安大略省　　rise (raɪz) *n.* 上升
destructive (dɪˈstrʌktɪv) *adj.* 破壞性的　　act (ækt) *n.* 行爲
suicide (ˈsuəˌsaɪd) *n.* 自殺

1. (**B**) 根據本文，天氣的改變

    (A) 是人們的行為所造成的。

    (B) <u>會影響人們的行為。</u>

    (C) 只在東京影響個人行為。

    (D) 只影響那些搭乘巴士和電車的人。

2. (**D**) 當東京的氣壓下降時，

    (A) 數以百計的人因掉落的瓦礫而受傷。

    (B) 人們的記憶力改善了。

    (C) 人們出門時總帶著傘。

    (D) <u>人們搭乘大眾運輸工具時容易遺忘東西。</u>

    * debris〔də'bri〕*n.* 瓦礫堆　　***tend to*** 容易
      transportation〔ˌtrænspɚ'teʃən〕*n.* 運輸工具

3. (**C**) 本文所提到的研究，都顯示出天氣改變時會產生的現象，以下何者
除外？

    (A) 暫時的健忘　　　　　　(B) 汽車駕駛人之間缺乏協調合作

    (C) <u>工作壓力的減少</u>　　　　(D) 自殺

    * ***all but~*** 除了~之外
      temporary〔'tɛmpəˌrɛrɪ〕*adj.* 暫時的
      coordination〔koˌɔrdn̩'eʃən〕*n.* 協調；合作

4. (**B**) 我們可以推論，當氣壓上升時，

    (A) 有更多的人會自殺。　　(B) <u>人們較能夠專心。</u>

    (C) 人們所承受的壓力較輕。　(D) 人們較不常開車。

5. (**D**) 安大略是什麼？

    (A) 是一個研究機構。　　　(B) 是氣壓計。

    (C) 是個都市。　　　　　　(D) <u>是加拿大的一省。</u>

    * institute〔'ɪnstəˌtjut〕*n.* 機構　　province〔'prɑvɪns〕*n.* 省

TEST 32

Read the following passage, and choose the best answer for each question.

The monster came toward us with twice our speed. We gasped in amazement. We were awed and silent. The animal came on, playing with the waves. It circled the Abraham Lincoln, then moved away two or three miles, leaving a bright wake. All at once it rushed from the dark horizon toward the ship with a frightening speed. When it was about twenty feet away, the light suddenly went out, and then appeared on the other side of us, as if the monster had gone beneath us.

1. In the above paragraph, what do you think the monster probably is?
   - (A) a ship
   - (B) a whale
   - (C) an elephant
   - (D) a giant wave

2. What does the name Abraham Lincoln stand for in this paragraph?
   - (A) an animal
   - (B) a big fish
   - (C) a ship
   - (D) a famous person

3. What is a wake?

    (A) It is a kind of light.

    (B) It is a path in the water.

    (C) It is a tail.

    (D) It is a monster.

4. How did the people feel?

    (A) They were overjoyed.

    (B) They were relaxed.

    (C) They were astounded.

    (D) They were aggressive.

5. At what time of day does this event take place?

    (A) It is midday.

    (B) It is morning.

    (C) It is night.

    (D) We cannot tell from the passage.

TEST 32 詳解

The monster came *toward us with twice our speed*. We gasped

in amazement. We were awed and silent. The animal came on,

playing with the waves. It circled the Abraham Lincoln, *then*

moved *away two or three miles, leaving a bright wake*.

那怪物以我們的兩倍速度向我們衝過來。我們嚇得倒抽一口氣,怕得不敢
吭聲。那怪物一直接近我們,戲弄著海浪,繞著林肯總統號,然後游到二、三
英哩外,留下一道明亮的水痕。

> monster (ˈmɑnstɚ) *n.* 怪物　　gasp (gæsp) *v.* (因驚訝而) 倒抽一口氣
> amazement (əˈmezmənt) *n.* 驚訝　　awed (ɔd) *adj.* 畏懼的
> circle (ˈsɝkḷ) *v.* 環繞　　wake (wek) *n.* (船經過時所留下的) 航跡

All at once it rushed *from the dark horizon toward the ship* with

a frightening speed. **When** *it was about twenty feet away*, the light

suddenly went out, **and** then appeared *on the other side of us, as*

if the monster had gone beneath us.

突然間它又以驚人的速度,從黑暗的地平線衝向船來。當它離船約二十英呎時,
光突然熄滅,然後又出現在我們另一邊,就好像那怪物就從我們船底下通過一
樣。

> all at once 突然間　　rush (rʌʃ) *v.* 衝
> horizon (həˈraɪzn) *n.* 地平線　　frightening (ˈfraɪtnɪŋ) *adj.* 驚人的
> go out 熄滅　　as if 就好像　　beneath (bɪˈniθ) *prep.* 在～下面

1. (**B**) 根據以上短文，你認為怪物可能是什麼？
   (A) 一艘船　　　　　　　　(B) 一隻鯨魚
   (C) 一頭大象　　　　　　　(D) 一股巨浪
   * whale〔hwel〕*n.* 鯨魚　　giant〔'dʒaɪənt〕*adj.* 巨大的

2. (**C**) 本文中，亞伯拉罕‧林肯這個名字代表什麼？
   (A) 一隻動物　　　　　　　(B) 一條大魚
   (C) 一艘船　　　　　　　　(D) 一位名人
   * *stand for* 代表

3. (**B**) "wake" 是什麼？
   (A) 是一種光。　　　　　　(B) 是製造痕跡者行經的路線。
   (C) 是一條尾巴。　　　　　(D) 是一個怪物。
   * path〔pæθ〕*n.* 路徑　　tail〔tel〕*n.* 尾巴

4. (**C**) 那些人覺得如何？
   (A) 非常高興。　　　　　　(B) 非常輕鬆。
   (C) 非常驚訝。　　　　　　(D) 非常積極。
   * overjoyed〔'ovə'dʒɔɪd〕*adj.* 非常高興的
     relaxed〔rɪ'lækst〕*adj.* 放鬆的
     astounded〔ə'staʊndɪd〕*adj.* 感到震驚的
     aggressive〔ə'grɛsɪv〕*adj.* 積極進取的；具攻擊性的

5. (**C**) 這件事發生在什麼時候？
   (A) 中午。　　　　　　　　(B) 早上。
   (C) 晚上。　　　　　　　　(D) 我們無法從本文判斷。
   * midday〔'mɪd,de〕*n.* 正午　　tell〔tɛl〕*v.* 判斷

TEST 33

Read the following passage, and choose the best answer for each question.

Jones College is a large school which not only boasts a beautiful campus, but is also surrounded by charming rural villages. It offers advantages, such as small classes, individual counseling and private dorm rooms, which few schools of its size can match. The college offers degrees in a wide range of liberal arts fields, though no longer in oriental languages, and has a wide-ranging sports program embracing most of the usual collegiate sports, with the exception of football. In contrast to nearby White College, which requires students to live off-campus, Jones houses all of its all-male student population in dormitories on campus.

1. Students at Jones College _____
   (A) enjoy fewer advantages than students at White College.
   (B) must live in the nearby towns.
   (C) do not know their classmates at all.
   (D) cannot learn Japanese at school.

2. Students at Jones College _____
   (A) love to play football.
   (B) cannot be women.
   (C) do not have a chance to study anything except science.
   (D) must have at least one roommate.

3. Jones College has ——————————

   (A) limits on the size of classes.
   (B) few dormitories.
   (C) few student services for a large school.
   (D) many students studying in scientific fields.

4. What is true about Jones College?

   (A) It is far away from White College.
   (B) It is the number one football rival of White College.
   (C) It has extensive university housing.
   (D) Its students are all women.

5. At Jones College students ——————————

   (A) must have a roommate.
   (B) must play football.
   (C) may live in a charming rural village.
   (D) may study French.

TEST 33 詳解

Jones College is a large school **which not only** boasts a
beautiful campus, **but** is **also** surrounded by charming rural villages.
It offers advantages, such as small classes, individual counseling
and private dorm rooms, **which** few schools of its size can match.

瓊斯學院是所大學校，不僅以擁有美麗的校園自豪，四周也被迷人的農莊
所圍繞。這個學院有很多優點，例如小班教學、個人諮詢，以及單人房宿舍等
等，這些都是其他同等規模的學校很少能比得上的。

> boast〔bost〕v. 以擁有～而自豪　　campus〔'kæmpəs〕n. 校園
> rural〔'rʊrəl〕adj. 農村的　　counseling〔'kaʊnslɪŋ〕n. 諮詢服務
> dorm〔dɔrm〕n. 宿舍〔= dormitory〕　　match〔mætʃ〕v. 比得上

The college offers degrees in a wide range of liberal arts fields,
though no longer in oriental languages, **and** has a wide-ranging
sports program embracing most of the usual collegiate sports, with
the exception of football.

在文理學科方面，它提供了範圍相當廣泛的學位，雖然不再包含東方語文的學
位，而且在各種體育課程中，也包含一般學院所提供的大部分運動，但美式足
球除外。

> * though no…languages 為副詞子句之插入語，省略了主詞和動詞。
> （詳見文寶典 p.653）

> degree〔dɪ'gri〕n. 學位　　range〔rendʒ〕n. 範圍　　v. 範圍包括
> **liberal arts** 文理科　　oriental〔ˌorɪ'ɛntḷ〕adj. 東方的
> program〔'progræm〕n. 課程　　embrace〔ɪm'bres〕v. 包含
> collegiate〔kə'lidʒɪɪt〕adj. 學院的

*In contrast to nearby White College, **which** requires students to live*

off-campus, Jones houses all of its all-male student population *in*

dormitories on campus.

瓊斯學院和附近的懷特學院所不同的是，後者要求學生住在校外，而前者則讓全校清一色的男生，全部都住在校內宿舍中。

> ***in contrast to~*** 與~形成對比；與~相反
> off-campus〔'ɔf'kæmpəs〕*adv.* 在校園外

1. (**D**) 瓊斯學院的學生
   (A) 比懷特學院的學生享有較少的好處。
   (B) 一定要住在附近的城鎮。
   (C) 完全不認識同學。　　(D) 無法在學校學日文。

2. (**B**) 瓊斯學院的學生
   (A) 熱愛美式足球。　　　(B) 不可能是女性。
   (C) 除了科學之外，無法研習其他學問。
   (D) 至少會有一位室友。

3. (**A**) 瓊斯學院
   (A) 限制班級的大小。　　(B) 宿舍很少。
   (C) 很少提供大型學校該有的學生服務。
   (D) 有許多學生研究科學。

4. (**C**) 下列有關瓊斯學院的敘述何者正確？
   (A) 離懷特學院很遠。　　(B) 是懷特學院頭號的美式足球對手。
   (C) 有大規模的學校宿舍。　(D) 學生都是女性。

5. (**D**) 瓊斯學院的學生
   (A) 必須有一位室友。　　(B) 必須要會打美式足球。
   (C) 可以住在迷人的農莊。　(D) 可以研讀法文。

TEST 34

Read the following passage, and choose the best answer for each question.

San Francisco is one of the most beautiful and unusual cities in the world, and it attracts a lot of tourists, both American and foreign, all year round. This fascinating town at the tip of the Californian peninsula is the western gateway of America. Historians call it "the city of the Golden Gate." Lovers call it "the city by the bay." Those who don't live there call it "Frisco." About one million people call it home. It was not until 1849 when the gold rush started in California that the town really began to grow. In fact, a year later, it became an incorporated city. The gold rush turned San Francisco into a boom town and established the basis for the city's later development into a major financial and cultural complex of America.

1. Without the gold rush, San Francisco would probably _____

    (A) never have existed.
    (B) be able to attract more tourists today.
    (C) not have prospered as it did.
    (D) have become the capital of the United States.

2. Tourists visit "the city of the Golden Gate" in _____
    (A) spring.　　　　　(B) summer.
    (C) autumn.　　　　　(D) every season of the year.

3. San Francisco has a population of about _____

    (A) one and a half million.

    (B) one million.

    (C) two million.

    (D) fifty hundred thousand.

4. "The western gateway of America" refers to _____

    (A) San Francisco.   (B) Los Angeles.

    (C) California.   (D) Seattle.

5. San Francisco became an incorporated city in _____

    (A) 1850.   (B) 1849.

    (C) 1847.   (D) 1851.

TEST 34 詳解

San Francisco is one of the most beautiful and unusual cities in the world, *and* it attracts a lot of tourists, both American and foreign, all year round. This fascinating town at the tip of the Californian peninsula is the western gateway of America.

舊金山是世界上最漂亮、最特殊的都市之一,它一年到頭吸引了很多的觀光客,包括美國人和外國人。這座位於加州半島尖端的迷人城市,是美國西部的門戶。

fascinating (ˈfæsn̩ˌetɪŋ) *adj.* 迷人的   tip (tɪp) *n.* 尖端
peninsula (pəˈnɪnsələ) *n.* 半島   gateway (ˈgetˌwe) *n.* 門戶;出入口

Historians call it "the city of the Golden Gate." Lovers call it "the city by the bay." Those who don't live there call it "Frisco." About one million people call it home. It was not until 1849 when the gold rush started in California that the town really began to grow.

歷史學家稱它為「金門灣的城市」。情侶稱它為「海灣邊的城市」。不住在那裏的人稱它為「三藩市」。大約一百萬人稱它為家。直到一八四九年,當加州掀起了淘金的熱潮時,這座城市才眞正開始發展。

* the city…Gate、the city…bay、Frisco 和 home 都是受詞補語,補充說明 it,it 是指 San Francisco。when…California 是形容詞子句,修飾 1849。

historian (hɪsˈtorɪən) *n.* 歷史學家   bay (be) *n.* 海灣
Frisco (ˈfrɪsko) *n.*(俗)舊金山;三藩市   rush (rʌʃ) *n.* 熱潮

In fact, a year later, it became an incorporated city. The gold

rush turned San Francisco into a boom town ***and*** established the

basis *for the city's later development into a major financial and*

cultural complex of America.

事實上，一年之後，它成為一座合併的城市。淘金的熱潮使得舊金山，漸漸成為繁榮的城市，而且為這城市，以後成為美國主要財政和文化中心的發展，建立了基礎。

> incorporated〔ɪn'kɔrpə,retɪd〕*adj.* 合併的
> boom〔bum〕*adj.* 繁榮的　complex〔'kɑmplɛks〕*n.* 綜合體

1. (**C**) 要是沒有淘金的熱潮，舊金山也許
   (A) 不會存在。
   (B) 今天可以吸引更多的觀光客。
   (C) 不會那樣的繁榮。
   (D) 已成為美國的首都。
   * prosper〔'prɑspɚ〕*v.* 繁榮　capital〔'kæpətḷ〕*n.* 首都

2. (**D**) 觀光客會在 _____ 拜訪「金門灣的城市」。
   (A) 春天　　　　　　　　(B) 夏天
   (C) 秋天　　　　　　　　(D) 一年中的每個季節

3. (**B**) 舊金山大約有 _____ 人口。
   (A) 一百五十萬　(B) 一百萬　(C) 二百萬　(D) 五十萬

4. (**A**) 「美國西部的門戶」是指
   (A) 舊金山。　(B) 洛杉磯。　(C) 加州。　(D) 西雅圖。

5. (**A**) 舊金山在 _____ 年成為一座合併的都市。
   (A) 一八五〇　(B) 一八四九　(C) 一八四七　(D) 一八五一

TEST 35

Refer to the following newspaper classified advertising index:

Auction	11
Automotive	13-14
Business Opportunities	17-18
Capital to Invest	19-20
Mortgages	16
Real Estate	15

1. On which of the pages of the newspaper would one look to find the information on car sales?

    (A) 11.   (B) 13-14.

    (C) 16.   (D) 17-18.

2. Which of the following pages would most likely contain a list of homes for sale?

    (A) 11.   (B) 15.

    (C) 16.   (D) 19.

3. On which of the pages would one find the information on purchasing a convertible or limousine?

    (A) 11.   (B) 13-14.

    (C) 16.   (D) 17-18.

4. Under which designation would one find information on loans?

   (A) Auction.
   (B) Business Opportunities.
   (C) Real Estate.
   (D) Mortgages.

5. On which page should you begin your research if you want to start your own business?

   (A) Auction.
   (B) Business Opportunities.
   (C) Real Estate.
   (D) Mortgages.

TEST 35 詳解

參考下列分類廣告的索引：

拍　　賣	11
汽　　車	13-14
生意機會	17-18
資金投資	19-20
抵押貸款	16
房 地 產	15

refer to 參考　　***classified advertising*** 分類廣告
index (ˋɪndɛks) *n.* 索引　　auction (ˋɔkʃən) *n.* 拍賣
automotive (ˏɔtəˋmotɪv) *adj.* 有關汽車的
capital (ˋkæpətḷ) *n.* 資金　　invest (ɪnˋvɛst) *v.* 投資
mortgage (ˋmɔrgɪdʒ) *n.* 抵押貸款　　***real estate*** 房地產

1. (**B**) 可以在報紙的哪一頁找到汽車出售的訊息？
   (A) 第 11 頁。　　　　　　(B) 第 13～14 頁。
   (C) 第 16 頁。　　　　　　(D) 第 17～18 頁。

2. (**B**) 下列哪一頁可能刊載房屋出售的廣告？
   (A) 第 11 頁。　　　　　　(B) 第 15 頁。
   (C) 第 16 頁。　　　　　　(D) 第 19 頁。

   * list (lɪst) *n.* 一覽表；名單
   home「家」是抽象名詞，但在房屋廣告中常代替 house。

3. (**B**) 可以在報紙的哪一頁，找到購買敞篷車或大型高級房車的訊息？

    (A) 第 11 頁。　　　　　　(B) <u>第 13～14 頁。</u>

    (C) 第 16 頁。　　　　　　(D) 第 17～18 頁。

    * purchase (ˋpɝtʃəs) v. 購買
      convertible (kənˋvɝtəbl̩) n. 敞篷車
      limousine (ˋlɪmə͵zin ͵͵lɪməˋzin) n. 大型高級房車；小型巴士

4. (**D**) 下列名稱中，何者可找到貸款的訊息？

    (A) 拍賣。　　　　　　　(B) 生意機會。

    (C) 房地產。　　　　　　(D) <u>抵押貸款。</u>

    * designation (͵dɛzɪgˋneʃen ͵dɛs -) n. 名稱

5. (**B**) 如果你想創業，應該找哪一頁開始你的研究？

    (A) 拍賣。　　　　　　　(B) <u>生意機會。</u>

    (C) 房地產。　　　　　　(D) 抵押貸款。

    * research (ˋrisɝtʃ) n. 研究

> 本書經過實際測驗研究，做到十回以後，你
> 的閱讀速度會逐漸加快，考試就不再怕閱讀
> 測驗了。

TEST 36

Read the following passage, and choose the best answer for each question.

To the curious and the courageous, the sea still presents the challenge of the unknown, for ignorance is still the distinguishing characteristic of man's relation to the sea. But now, more than ever, necessity goads us onward in our exploration of the sea. We now have submarines, capable of steady submergence for many months, holding missiles capable of destruction many times greater than those used in World War II. For strategic reasons, therefore, we need urgently to learn more about the ocean bottom. Quite apart from the threat of war, another necessity pressed us to learn to master the sea. The necessity is basic to life itself: food. The lives of two-thirds of the world's people are wholly dictated by that basic necessity; they are oppressed by hunger and by the weakness and disease which hunger generates. Out of the sea we can extract the food to relieve the hunger of these millions of people and give dignity to their lives. We must turn to the sea, because the bounty of the land has limits.

1. Apart from strategic considerations, we need to conquer the sea to solve the problem of _____
   (A) food supply.   (B) population explosion.
   (C) environmental pollution.   (D) wildlife conservation.

2. Which of the following statements is true?

(A) The whole world population is suffering from hunger.

(B) The greatest waste in food consumption is brought about by the creatures from the ocean.

(C) Conquering the sea may ultimately mean the conquest of the world which has always been man's sole ambition.

(D) The ocean may hold the key to solving the world's food problem.

3. Wisely explored and fairly distributed of its harvests, the sea stands for _____

(A) a mighty threat.

(B) an unseen enemy.

(C) a great challenge.

(D) a potential promise.

4. According to the passage, which of the following statements is true?

(A) The sea presents few difficulties to man.

(B) The average man can read the sea like a map.

(C) As yet, we don't know well enough about the sea.

(D) It is only the curious and the courageous that reject taking up the challenge of exploring the sea.

5. Modern submarines can _____

(A) destroy all the natural resources at the ocean bottom.

(B) stay under water for months without returning to their base for supplies.

(C) be the one and only answer to win the next war.

(D) be economically used as transport vessels to ferry enormous quantities of strategic metals mined from the ocean floor.

TEST 36 詳解

To the curious and the courageous, the sea *still* presents the challenge *of the unknown, **for** ignorance is still the distinguishing characteristic of man's relation to the sea. **But** now, more than ever,* necessity goads us *onward in our exploration of the sea.*

對於好奇者和勇者而言，海洋仍是個未知的挑戰，因為不熟悉仍然是人類和海洋關係的顯著特徵。但是現在，更甚於以往，需要驅使我們，更進一步去探究海洋。

courageous (kəˈredʒəs) *adj.* 勇敢的　　present (prɪˈzɛnt) *v.* 呈現
ignorance (ˈɪgnərəns) *n.* 無知；不熟悉
distinguishing (dɪˈstɪŋgwɪʃɪŋ) *adj.* 顯著的
characteristic (ˌkærɪktəˈrɪstɪk) *n.* 特徵
goad (god) *v.* 驅使　　onward (ˈɑnwəd) *adv.* 向前
exploration (ˌɛkspləˈreʃən) *n.* 探險；研究

We *now* have submarines *(**which** are) capable of steady submergence for many months holding missiles (**which** are) capable of destruction many times greater **than** those used in World War II.*

我們現有的潛水艇，能夠持續好幾個月潛在水底，所攜帶的飛彈，其破壞力比第二次世界大戰所使用的那些大許多倍。

submarine (ˈsʌbməˌrin) *n.* 潛水艇　　***be capable of*** 能夠
steady (ˈstɛdɪ) *adj.* 持續的
submergence (səbˈmɝdʒəns) *n.* 沉入水中；潛水
missile (ˈmɪsḷ) *n.* 飛彈　　destruction (dɪˈstrʌkʃən) *n.* 破壞

For strategic reasons, therefore, we need *urgently* to learn more

about the ocean bottom.

因此，為了戰略上的理由，我們迫切需要學習更多有關海底的事物。

strategic〔strəˈtidʒɪk〕*adj.* 戰略的　　urgently〔ˈɝdʒətlɪ〕*adv.* 迫切地
bottom〔ˈbɑtəm〕*n.* 底部

Quite apart from the threat of war, another necessity pressed us to

learn to master the sea. The necessity is basic to life itself: food.

除了戰爭的威脅外，有另一種需要迫使我們去學習支配海洋。那種需要對生命
本身是基本的：食物。

* Quite…war 是副詞片語，修飾全句；to learn…sea 是不定詞片語，作受
　詞補語。句中的支點（：）是介紹單字以加強語氣（詳見文法寶典 p.42）。

apart from 除了～之外　　threat〔θrɛt〕*n.* 威脅
master〔ˈmæstɚ〕*v.* 支配；控制
be basic to 對～而言是基本的

The lives *of two-thirds of the world's people* are *wholly* dictated *by*

that basic necessity; they are oppressed *by hunger and by the weak-*

ness and disease **which hunger generates.**

全世界有三分之二的人，受到這種基本的需要所左右；他們受到饑餓，和因饑
餓所產生的虛弱和疾病所壓迫。

* of…people 是形容詞片語，修飾 lives；which 引導的形容詞子句，修飾
　weakness 及 disease。

dictate〔ˈdɪktet〕*v.* 命令　　oppress〔əˈprɛs〕*v.* 壓迫
generate〔ˈdʒɛnəˌret〕*v.* 產生

Out of the sea we can extract the food *to relieve the hunger of*

these millions of people **and** *give dignity to their lives.* We must

turn to the sea, ***because** the bounty of the land has limits*.

從海洋中，我們可以取得食物，以消除好幾百萬人的饑餓，讓他們活得有尊嚴。
我們必須求助於海洋，因為陸地所能給予我們的東西是有限的。

> * Out…sea 是副詞片語，修飾 extract，表地方；to relieve…and give…
> 是由 and 所連接的兩個不定詞片語，當副詞用，修飾 extract，表目的。
> because 引導副詞子句，修飾 turn，表原因。

> extract (ɪkˈstrækt) *v.* 取得　　relieve (rɪˈliv) *v.* 解除；減輕
> dignity (ˈdɪgnətɪ) *n.* 尊嚴　　***turn to*** 求助於
> bounty (ˈbauntɪ) *n.* 施與；恩賜

1. (**A**) 除了戰略的考量外，我們必須征服海洋，以解決 ＿＿＿＿＿＿ 的問題。

　　(A) 食物供給　　　　　　　　(B) 人口爆炸
　　(C) 環境污染　　　　　　　　(D) 保護野生動物

> * conquer (ˈkɑŋkɚ) *v.* 征服　　explosion (ɪkˈsploʒən) *n.* 爆炸
> wildlife (ˈwaɪld,laɪf) *n.* 野生動物
> conservation (,kɑnsɚˈveʃən) *n.* 保護；保存

2. (**D**) 下列敘述何者正確？

　　(A) 全世界的人都受饑餓之苦。
　　(B) 食物消耗最大的浪費是由海洋生物所引起的。
　　(C) 征服海洋最後可能意謂著征服世界，這一向是人類唯一的抱負。
　　(D) 海洋可能掌握解決全世界食物問題的關鍵。

> * consumption (kənˈsʌmpʃən) *n.* 消耗　　***bring about*** 導致；造成
> creature (ˈkritʃɚ) *n.* 生物　　ultimately (ˈʌltəmɪtlɪ) *adv.* 最後
> conquest (ˈkɑŋkwɛst) *n.* 征服　　sole (sol) *adj.* 唯一的
> ambition (æmˈbɪʃən) *n.* 抱負　　key (ki) *n.* 關鍵

3. (**D**) 若能明智地探究，並且公平地分配其收穫，則海洋可代表

(A) 一個強大的威脅。　　(B) 一個看不見的敵人。

(C) 一個極大的挑戰。　　(D) <u>一個潛在的希望。</u>

　* *stand for* 代表　　mighty ('maɪtɪ) *adj.* 強大的
　　potential (pə'tɛnʃəl) *adj.* 潛在的　　promise ('prɑmɪs) *n.* 希望

4. (**C**) 根據本文，下列敘述何者正確？

(A) 海洋對人類而言沒什麼困難。

(B) 一般人對海洋非常了解。

(C) <u>到目前爲止，我們對海洋所知仍然不足。</u>

(D) 只有好奇者和勇者拒絕接受海洋探險的挑戰。

　* *as yet* 到目前爲止
　　read~like a map 對~非常了解 (= *read~like a book*)

5. (**B**) 現代的潛水艇能夠

(A) 破壞所有海底的天然資源。

(B) <u>停留在海底好幾個月，不必回到基地補給。</u>

(C) 成爲贏得下次戰爭的唯一方法。

(D) 十分經濟地被用作運輸艦，以載運自海底開採出的大量戰略金屬。

　* *natural resources* 天然資源　　base (bes) *n.* 基地
　　transport (træns'port) *n.* 運輸　　vessel ('vɛsḷ) *n.* 船；艦
　　ferry ('fɛrɪ) *v.* 載運　　enormous (ɪ'nɔrməs) *adj.* 極大的
　　metal ('mɛtḷ) *n.* 金屬　　mine (maɪn) *v.* 開採

TEST 37

Read the following passage, and choose the best answer for each question.

A new project is being set up to discover the best ways of sorting and separating garbage. When this project is complete, garbage will be processed like this: first, it will pass through sharp metal spikes which will tear open the plastic bags in which garbage is usually packed; then it will pass through a powerful fan to separate the lightest elements from the heavy solids; after that crushers and rollers will break up everything that can be broken. Finally, the garbage will pass under magnets, which will remove the bits of iron and steel; the rubber and plastic will then be sorted out in the final stage.

The first full-scale giant recycling plants are, perhaps, years away. But in some big industrial areas, where garbage has been dumped for so long that there are no holes left to fill up with garbage, these new automatic recycling plants may be built sooner. Indeed, with the growing cost of transporting garbage to more distant dumps, some big cities will be forced to build their own recycling plants before long.

1. When this project is complete, plants will be built for _____
   - (A) storing garbage.
   - (B) dumping garbage.
   - (C) the petrochemical industries.
   - (D) the recycling of waste.

2. Then, because everything which goes into the garbage can would be made into something useful, the word garbage could _____
   - (A) last forever.
   - (B) revive.
   - (C) lose its meaning.
   - (D) come back to life.

3. Crushers and rollers are used to _____
   - (A) separate the light elements.
   - (B) reduce items to small pieces.
   - (C) tear open the plastic bags.
   - (D) remove the sharp metal spikes.

4. The full-scale giant plants could not be built perhaps until many years later, but the big cities may speed up the projects out of _____
   - (A) money.
   - (B) necessaries.
   - (C) necessity.
   - (D) curiosity.

5. Among the problems big cities face, an essential one is that _____
   - (A) there are too many holes.
   - (B) there is an acute labor shortage.
   - (C) moving garbage to faraway dumps is too costly.
   - (D) finding the right man for the right job is difficult.

TEST 37 詳解

A new project is being set up *to discover the best ways of sorting **and** separating garbage.*

　　一項新計劃正被擬定，以研究分類垃圾最好的方法。

* to discover…garbage 為不定詞片語當副詞用，修飾 set，表目的。

> project (ˈprɑdʒɛkt) *n.* 計劃　　***set up*** 建立　　sort (sɔrt) *v.* 分類
> separate (ˈsɛpəˌret) *v.* 分開；予以分類　　garbage (ˈgɑrbɪdʒ) *n.* 垃圾

***When** this project is complete,* garbage will be processed *like this*: *first*, it will pass through sharp metal spikes ***which** will tear open the plastic bags in **which** garbage is usually packed*; *then* it will pass through a powerful fan *to separate the lightest elements from the heavy solids*; *after that* crushers and rollers will break up everything ***that** can be broken.*

當這計劃完成的時候，垃圾的處理方式如下：首先，垃圾須經過尖銳的金屬長釘，將裝垃圾的塑膠袋撕開；接著會通過強有力的風扇，將較輕的物質與較重的固體分開；然後經壓碎機和輾壓機，就會弄碎所有可擊碎的東西。

* When 引導副詞子句，修飾 processed，表時間。first…broken 為三個對等子句，分別由分號（；）分開，第一個子句中 which will…packed 為形容詞子句，修飾 spikes，其中又有另一個形容詞子句 in which…packed，修飾 bags；第二個子句中 to separate…solids 為不定詞片語當副詞用，修飾 pass，表目的；第三個子句中 that can be broken 為形容詞子句，修飾 everything。

process ('prɑsɛs) *v.* 處理　　spike (spaɪk) *n.* 長釘

plastic ('plæstɪk) *adj.* 塑膠的　*n.* 塑膠

pack (pæk) *v.* 包裝　　tear (tɛr) *v.* 撕裂　　fan (fæn) *n.* 扇

solid ('sɑlɪd) *n.* 固體　　crusher ('krʌʃɚ) *n.* 壓碎機

roller ('rolɚ) *n.* 輾壓機；滾筒　　***break up*** 擊碎；破壞

Finally, the garbage will pass under magnets, ***which** will remove the bits of iron and steel*; the rubber and plastic will *then* be sorted out *in the final stage*.

最後垃圾將通過磁鐵，磁鐵會吸去鐵和鋼的碎片；然後橡膠和塑膠會在最後的階段被分類。

* which 引導補述用法的形容詞子句，補充說明 magnets。in the final stage 是副詞片語，修飾 sorted。

magnet ('mægnɪt) *n.* 磁鐵　　bit (bɪt) *n.* 碎屑

iron ('aɪɚn) *n.* 鐵　　steel (stil) *n.* 鋼

rubber ('rʌbɚ) *n.* 橡膠　　stage (stedʒ) *n.* 階段

The first full-scale giant recycling plants are, *perhaps*, years away. ***But** in some big industrial areas, **where** garbage has been dumped for **so** long **that** there are no holes left to fill up with garbage*, these new automatic recycling plants may be built *sooner*.

第一個全面性龐大的資源回收廠，或許是幾年以後的事了。但是在一些大型工業區，這些新的自動資源回收廠可能會較快完成，因為垃圾已經傾倒了很久，以致於再也沒有剩餘的坑洞來掩埋垃圾了。

* perhaps 是插入的副詞,修飾全句。But 是轉承語,連接前面的句子。where garbage…with garbage 是補述用法的形容詞子句,補充說明先行詞 areas,其中 so~that「如此~以致於」是從屬連接詞,so 是副詞,修飾 long,that…garbage 是副詞子句,修飾 so,表結果。(詳見文法寶典 p.516)

full-scale ('fʊl'skel) *adj.* 全面性的	giant ('dʒaɪənt) *adj.* 巨大的
recycle (,ri'saɪkl) *v.* 回收;再利用	plant (plænt) *n.* 工廠
industrial (ɪn'dʌstrɪəl) *adj.* 工業的	dump (dʌmp) *v.* 傾倒(垃圾)
hole (hol) *n.* 坑洞　　***fill up*** 填滿	

Indeed, with the growing cost of transporting garbage to more

distant dumps, some big cities will be forced to build their own

recycling plants *before long*.

的確,隨著運送垃圾到較遠的垃圾場去的費用漸增,有些大城市,不久將被迫,要建造他們自己的資源回收廠。

* Indeed「的確」是副詞,修飾全句。with…dumps 是副詞片語,修飾 forced。before long 是副詞片語,修飾 forced,表時間。

transport (træns'port) *v.* 運送	distant ('dɪstənt) *adj.* 遙遠的
dump (dʌmp) *n.* 垃圾場	force (fors) *v.* 強迫　　***before long*** 不久

1. (**D**) 當這個計畫完成時,將會建一些 ＿＿＿＿＿＿ 的工廠。

    (A) 貯藏垃圾　　　　　　　(B) 傾倒垃圾

    (C) 石化工業　　　　　　　(D) 回收廢物

    * petrochemical (,pɛtro'kɛməkl) *adj.* 石油化學的
      waste (west) *n.* 廢物;廢料

2. (**C**) 因為每樣垃圾都會被處理成有用的東西,垃圾這個名詞到時候將會

    (A) 永遠持續。　　　　　　(B) 復活。

    (C) 失去意義。　　　　　　(D) 復活。

    * revive (rɪ'vaɪv) *v.* 復活(= *come back to life*)

3. (**B**) 壓碎機和輾壓機是用來

(A) 分離輕的物質。　　　　(B) <u>把每樣東西變成小碎片。</u>

(C) 撕開塑膠袋。　　　　　(D) 除去尖銳的金屬長釘。

* remove〔rɪ'muv〕*v.* 除去

4. (**C**) 全面性的大型工廠，或許要到許多年以後才會建好，但是大城市

可能為了 ＿＿＿＿＿＿＿ 而加速計畫的完成。

(A) 錢　　　　　　　　　　(B) 生活必需品

(C) <u>需要</u>　　　　　　　　　(D) 好奇

* necessaries〔'nɛsəˌsɛrɪz〕*n.pl.* 生活必需品

necessity〔nə'sɛsətɪ〕*n.* 必要；（迫切）需要

5. (**C**) 在大都市所面臨的問題中，最重要的一個是

(A) 有太多坑洞。

(B) 勞工嚴重短缺。

(C) <u>把垃圾運送到遠方的垃圾場費用太貴。</u>

(D) 找適合的人做適當的工作很困難。

* essential〔ɪ'sɛnʃəl〕*adj.* 非常重要的

acute〔ə'kjut〕*adj.* 嚴重的　　labor〔'lebɚ〕*n.* 勞工

shortage〔'ʃɔrtɪdʒ〕*n.* 短缺

faraway〔'fɑrəˌwe〕*adj.* 遙遠的

costly〔'kɔstlɪ〕*adj.* 昂貴的　　right〔raɪt〕*adj.* 適合的

TEST 38

Read the following passage, and choose the best answer for each question.

The most exciting question of all is, does life exist beyond
the earth? In recent years the trend has been toward the
hypothesis that life is probably a normal phenomenon wherever
the conditions are right, with the added qualification that
proper conditions are not necessarily only those of the earth.
It was long held, for example, that life on the planet Jupiter is
impossible because of its extreme cold, crushing gravity and
poisonous atmosphere. But there is evidence that the giant
planet is warmer below the outer, cold layers than was first
thought. The combination of gases in its atmosphere could
produce organic or preorganic molecules. Since no one really
knows all combinations of conditions under which life can
evolve, it is best to be conservative about denying the existence
of life on any planet.

1. Life on the planet Jupiter is a possibility which _____
    (A) does not exist.
    (B) should not be ruled out.
    (C) excites all scientists.
    (D) has never been explored.

2. Since we do not know all combinations of conditions under which life can develop, it is safer, the author advises, _____

   (A) to be conservative in asserting the existence of extraterrestrial life.

   (B) to take an aggressive attitude in denying the existence of life in space.

   (C) not to be too rash in dismissing the existence of life beyond the earth.

   (D) not to express one's opinion too clearly.

3. Life on other planets is possible _____

   (A) when life-evolving conditions exist.

   (B) only when their conditions match those of the earth.

   (C) when the temperature is neither too hot nor too cold.

   (D) when the atmosphere is not too dry.

4. According to the author, whether there is life beyond the earth is _____

   (A) the only question that excites people.

   (B) one of several questions which excite people.

   (C) one of the most exciting questions.

   (D) the question which excites people the most.

5. When we add qualifications to a condition, we _____

   (A) give a higher quality to the condition.

   (B) restrict and limit the condition.

   (C) remove all restrictions on condition.

   (D) enlarge the applicability of the condition.

TEST 38 詳解

The *most* exciting question *of all* is, does life exist *beyond*

the earth? *In recent years* the trend has been toward the hypothesis

that life *is* probably a normal phenomenon *wherever* the conditions

are right, with the added qualification *that* proper conditions are

not necessarily only those of the earth.

　　所有問題中，最令人感興趣的，就是地球之外，有沒有生物存在？最近幾年的趨勢，是傾向於只要條件適宜，生物就可能是一種正常現象這樣的假設，所附加的條件是，合適的條件並不一定只限於地球上的那些而已。

* does…earth 是以疑問句的形式，作主詞補語。that…earth 是名詞子句，作 hypothesis 的同位語，其中 wherever 引導表讓步的副詞子句，修飾 is。with…earth 是形容詞片語修飾 hypothesis，其中 that…earth 是名詞子句，作 qualification 的同位語。

　　　exist〔ɪg'zɪst〕*v.* 存在　　　life〔laɪf〕*n.* 生物
　　　trend〔trɛnd〕*n.* 趨勢
　　　hypothesis〔haɪ'pɑθəsɪs〕*n.* 假設
　　　phenomenon〔fə'namə,nan〕*n.* 現象
　　　conditions〔kən'dɪʃənz〕*n.pl.* 條件；環境
　　　qualification〔,kwɑləfə'keʃən〕*n.* 條件

It was *long* held, *for example*, *that* life *on the planet Jupiter is*

impossible *because of its extreme cold, crushing gravity and*

poisonous *atmosphere.*

例如，長久以來大家都認為，由於木星上非常寒冷，有令人受不了的重力，以及有毒的空氣，所以不可能有生物存在。

　　* It was long held that…是作客觀說明時的被動語態。

　　　　hold〔hold〕*v.* 認為　　　planet〔'plænɪt〕*n.* 行星
　　　　Jupiter〔'dʒupətɚ〕*n.* 木星
　　　　extreme〔ɪk'strim〕*adj.* 非常的
　　　　crushing〔'krʌʃɪŋ〕*adj.* 使人受不了的
　　　　gravity〔'grævətɪ〕*n.* 重力；地心引力
　　　　poisonous〔'pɔɪznəs〕*adj.* 有毒的
　　　　atmosphere〔'ætməs͵fɪr〕*n.* 空氣；大氣

But there is evidence ***that*** the giant planet is warmer below the outer, cold layers ***than*** was first thought. The combination of gases in its atmosphere could produce organic or preorganic molecules.
但是有證據顯示，這個巨大的行星，在外圍冷氣層的底下部分，比我們最初所想像的要溫暖。在木星大氣層裏的氣體組合，可產生有機物或成為有機物之前的分子。

　　* that 所引導的名詞子句，作 evidence 的同位語。below…layers 是形容詞片語，修飾 planet，因為太長，所以調到後面，使主詞和動詞靠近；than 引導表比較的副詞子句，修飾 warmer，子句中因為前後主詞相同，而省略主詞 the giant planet。

　　　　evidence〔'ɛvədəns〕*n.* 證據
　　　　giant〔'dʒaɪənt〕*adj.* 巨大的　　　layer〔'leɚ〕*n.* 層
　　　　combination〔͵kɑmbə'neʃən〕*n.* 混合
　　　　organic〔ɔr'gænɪk〕*adj.* 有機的
　　　　molecule〔'mɑlə͵kjul〕*n.* 分子
　　　　preorganic〔͵priɔr'gænɪk〕*adj.* 成為有機物之前的

Since *no one really knows all combinations of conditions under*

which *life can evolve*, it is best to be conservative about denying

the existence *of life on any planet.*

既然沒有人眞正知道，生物可以進化之條件的所有組合，那麼對於否認任何行星上有生命存在的這件事，最好還是保守一點。

* Since…evolve 是表原因的副詞子句，修飾 is。under which…evolve 是形容詞子句，修飾 conditions。it 是形式主詞，眞正主詞是後面不定詞片語 to be…planet；denying…planet 是名詞片語，作 about 的受詞。

evolve (ɪ'vɑlv) *v.* 進化
conservative (kən'sɝvətɪv) *adj.* 保守的
deny (dɪ'naɪ) *v.* 否認 existence (ɪg'zɪstəns) *n.* 存在

1. (**B**) 木星上有生物的可能性
   (A) 並不存在。   (B) 不該被排除。
   (C) 令所有科學家興奮。 (D) 尚未被探討。

   * *rule out* 排除 explore (ɪk'splor) *v.* 探討；探索

2. (**C**) 既然我們不知道生物可以進化之條件的所有組合，作者建議較保險的做法是
   (A) 保守地斷言地球以外有生物存在。
   (B) 抱持積極的態度否認太空中有生物的存在。
   (C) 不要過於輕率，認爲地球以外不會有生物的存在。
   (D) 不要太明確地表達個人的意見。

   * assert (ə'sɝt) *v.* 斷言
   extraterrestrial (ˌɛkstrətə'rɛstrɪəl) *adj.* 地球以外的
   aggressive (ə'grɛsɪv) *adj.* 積極的
   rash (ræʃ) *adj.* 輕率的 dismiss (dɪs'mɪs) *v.* 不予考慮

3. (**A**) ＿＿＿＿＿＿＿ 其他行星上有生物的存在是有可能的。

    (A) 當生物進化條件存在時，

    (B) 只有在環境和地球上的相符合時，

    (C) 當溫度既不太熱也不太冷時，

    (D) 當空氣不會太乾燥時，

    * match (mætʃ) v. 符合

4. (**D**) 根據作者的說法，地球外是否有生物是

    (A) 唯一使人們感興趣的問題。

    (B) 幾個使人們感興趣的問題之一。

    (C) 最令人感興趣的問題之一。

    (D) 最令人感興趣的問題。

5. (**B**) 當我們把條件加入一個情況中，我們

    (A) 給予這種情況更高的品質。

    (B) 約束並限制了這個情況。

    (C) 排除這情況的所有限制。

    (D) 擴大這情況的適用性。

    * restrict (rɪˋstrɪkt) v. 約束；限制

    restriction (rɪˋstrɪkʃən) n. 限制

    applicability (ˌæplɪkəˋbɪlətɪ) n. 適用性

    ※ 這條題目，參加「全國高中英文閱讀測驗大賽」的同學，大多選 (D)。

TEST 39

Read the following passage, and choose the best answer for each question.

Reading is like riding a bicycle. You don't read everything at the same speed. How fast you read often depends upon your reason for reading. Sometimes you need to read slowly and carefully. You do this when you study. You also read slowly when you are following a set of directions.

Sometimes you don't want to read a whole article or story. You may just be looking for a fact you need to know. Or you might be looking for the answer to a question. When you read very quickly for such a purpose, you are skimming. The article you are reading may have subheads or less important titles. You can use these to help you find the part of the article you want.

Other times you may be reading for fun. You read most fiction this way. You don't have to remember facts or ideas, so you read fairly quickly. You often need to read such stories only once.

1. This article compares reading to riding a bicycle because _____
   (A) reading is as much a pleasure as riding a bicycle.
   (B) you vary speeds in reading as well as in riding a bicycle.
   (C) you should read as fast as you ride a bicycle.
   (D) you must read slowly as you ride a bicycle slowly
       for safety.

2. You skim when you _____
   (A) don't want to know all the details of a whole article or story.
   (B) are following a set of directions.
   (C) are studying for exams.
   (D) ignore the subheads of an article.

3. When you read stories for fun, you generally read them _____
   (A) very carefully.   (B) many times.
   (C) rather slowly.   (D) no more than one time.

4. Which one of the following is one way of skimming?
   (A) Reading carefully.   (B) Reading slowly.
   (C) Memorizing something. (D) Reading subheads.

5. When you read fiction for fun, you should _____
   (A) skim because the details are not important anyway.
   (B) read carefully because many things in fiction are not true.
   (C) read quickly because it is not necessary to remember
       the details.
   (D) read it quickly so that you only have to read it once.

TEST 39 詳解

Reading is like riding a bicycle. You don't read everything *at the same speed*. ***How*** *fast you read often* depends upon your reason *for reading*. *Sometimes* you need to read *slowly and carefully*. You do this ***when*** *you study*. You *also* read *slowly* ***when*** *you are following a set of directions*.

閱讀就像騎腳踏車。你並非以同樣的速度閱讀每樣東西。閱讀的速度要多快，須依你的閱讀動機而定。有時候，你需要讀得慢而且仔細，譬如在用功唸書時。另外，在遵循一些指示說明時，也會讀得很慢。

> ***depend upon*** 視～而定　　directions (dəˈrɛkʃənz) *n. pl.* 指示；說明

Sometimes you don't want to read a whole article or story. You may *just* be looking for a fact *you need to know*. ***Or*** you might be looking for the answer *to a question*. ***When*** *you read very quickly for such a purpose*, you are skimming. The article *you are reading* may have subheads or *less* important titles. You can use these *to help you find the part of the article you want*.

有時候，你不會想讀完整篇文章或小說。你可以只找你需要知道的事實，或者，你可以只尋找某個問題的答案。當你為了此種目的而快速閱讀時，你其實是在略讀。你讀的文章裏面也許有小標題，或較不重要的標題，你可以利用這些，來幫助你找到文章中你想要看的部分。

> story (ˈstɔrɪ) *n.* 短篇小說　　skim (skɪm) *v.* 略讀
> subhead (ˈsʌbˌhɛd) *n.* 副標題　　title (ˈtaɪtl̩) *n.* 標題

Other times you may be reading *for fun*. You read most fiction *this way*. You don't have to remember facts or ideas, *so* you read *fairly quickly*. You *often* need to read such stories *only once*.

有時候，你可能只是爲了好玩而讀。讀小說時大多是如此。你不必記一些事實或觀念，所以可以讀得很快。通常這種小說只需要讀一次即可。

fiction (ˈfɪkʃən) *n.* 小說（集合名詞）　　fairly (ˈfɛrlɪ) *adv.* 相當地

1. (**B**) 本文將閱讀比喻成騎腳踏車，是因爲
   (A) 閱讀與騎腳踏車一樣有趣。
   (B) 閱讀和騎腳踏車一樣，可以調整速度。
   (C) 閱讀要和騎腳踏車一樣快。
   (D) 爲了確保安全，閱讀要和騎腳踏車一樣慢。
   * compare (kəmˈpɛr) *v.* 比喻成　　vary (ˈvɛrɪ) *v.* 改變

2. (**A**) 當你 ＿＿＿＿＿＿ 時，你會略讀。
   (A) 不想知道整篇文章或小說的細節
   (B) 遵循一些指示說明
   (C) 爲考試而研讀　　　　　　　　(D) 忽略文章的小標題

3. (**D**) 當你爲了好玩而閱讀小說時，你通常
   (A) 讀得很仔細。　(B) 讀好幾次。　(C) 讀得很慢。　(D) 只讀一次。

4. (**D**) 下列何者是略讀的方式之一？
   (A) 讀得很仔細。　(B) 讀得很慢。　(C) 背誦事物。　(D) 讀小標題。
   * memorize (ˈmɛməˌraɪz) *v.* 背誦

5. (**C**) 當你爲了好玩而讀小說時，你應該
   (A) 略讀，反正細節並不重要。
   (B) 要仔細讀，因爲小說裡有很多事都是虛構的。
   (C) 讀快一點，因爲不需要去記其中的細節。
   (D) 讀快一點，這樣就只需要讀一遍。

TEST 40

Read the following passage, and choose the best answer for each question.

OFFICE SPACE AVAILABLE

We have for lease carpeted, air-conditioned offices on the third floor of the Post-Intelligencer Building. Some offices with window views, all ready for immediate occupancy.

All utilities furnished, including janitor service and nightly / weekend security service.

Also includes parking, cafeteria, conference facilities, two passenger elevators and a freight elevator.

Building is within easy walking distance of stores, restaurants, bus service, Seattle City Center, and has easy access to the freeway.

For further information call Gary Walden at 628-8097.

---

1. The offices in the advertisement are for
   (A) sale.   (B) mortgage.
   (C) rent.   (D) auction.

2. All the offices advertised on the third floor of the Post-Intelligencer Building have
   (A) window views.
   (B) their own elevators.
   (C) carpet and air conditioning.
   (D) 24-hour security.

3. The Post-Intelligencer Building has a
   (A) restaurant.   (B) store.
   (C) cafeteria.   (D) resident security guard.

4. The Seattle City Center is
   (A) close by.
   (B) next door.
   (C) near the freeway.
   (D) a long distance from the Post-Intelligencer Building.

5. People who wish to lease office space in the Post-
   Intelligencer Building must
   (A) supply their own security service.
   (B) visit Gary Walden.
   (C) wish to use conference facilities.
   (D) call 628-8097.

TEST 40 詳解

辦 公 室 出 租

舖有地毯、有空調的辦公室出租，位郵情大樓三樓。有些辦公室窗戶可瀏覽外景。可立即遷入使用。

公共設施完善，包括管理服務、週末及夜間警衛服務。

還有停車場、自助餐廳、會議設備、兩台供人搭乘電梯，以及一台載貨電梯。

商店、餐廳、巴士站、西雅圖市中心，步行可達，且近高速公路。

詳情電 628-8097 葛雷・華登。

---

lease〔lis〕*n.,v.* 出租　　carpet〔'kɑrpɪt〕*v.* 鋪設地毯

air-conditioned〔'ɛrkən'dɪʃənd〕*adj.* 有空調設備的

occupancy〔'ɑkjəpənsɪ〕*n.* 占有；居住

utilities〔ju'tɪlətɪz〕*n.pl.* 公共設施（如水、電、瓦斯等）

furnish〔'fɝnɪʃ〕*v.* 裝設；供給　　janitor〔'dʒænətə〕*n.* 管理員

security〔sɪ'kjurətɪ〕*n.* 安全　　cafeteria〔ˌkæfə'tɪrɪə〕*n.* 自助餐廳

conference〔'kɑnfərəns〕*n.* 會議　　facilities〔fə'sɪlətɪz〕*n.pl.* 設備

passenger〔'pæsṇdʒə〕*n.* 乘客　　elevator〔'ɛləˌvetə〕*n.* 電梯

freight〔fret〕*n.* 運貨；貨物　　Seattle〔si'ætḷ〕*n.* 西雅圖

have easy access to 易於接近　　further〔'fɝðə〕*adj.* 更進一步的

1. (**C**) 廣告中的辦公室是要

　　(A) 出售。　　　　　　　　　(B) 貸款。

　　(C) 出租。　　　　　　　　　(D) 拍賣。

　　* advertisement〔ˌædvə'taɪzmənt〕*n.* 廣告

　　mortgage〔'mɔrgɪdʒ〕*n.* 貸款；抵押

　　auction〔'ɔkʃən〕*n.* 拍賣

2. (**C**) 廣告刊登郵情大樓三樓所有的辦公室都有

　　(A) 瀏覽戶外景色的窗子。

　　(B) 自己的電梯。

　　(C) <u>地毯和空調設備。</u>

　　(D) 二十四小時警衛。

　　* *air conditioning* 冷氣設備

3. (**C**) 郵情大樓有

　　(A) 餐廳。　　　　　　　(B) 商店。

　　(C) <u>自助餐廳。</u>　　　　(D) 住在大樓內的警衛。

　　* resident ('rɛzədənt) *adj.* 長駐的；居住的

4. (**A**) 西雅圖市中心

　　(A) <u>在附近。</u>　　　　　(B) 在隔壁。

　　(C) 靠近高速公路。　　　(D) 離郵情大樓很遠。

5. (**D**) 想租郵情大樓辦公室的人必須

　　(A) 自己提供安全服務。

　　(B) 拜訪葛雷・華登。

　　(C) 希望使用會議設備。

　　(D) <u>打 628-8097。</u>

TEST 41

Read the following passage, and choose the best answer for each question.

"Memorize these words." "Learn this spelling rule." "Don't forget the quiz tomorrow." You remember things every day, but how do you do it?

You find a telephone number in the phone book, dial it, and then forget it. This is your short-term memory. It lasts less than 30 seconds. However, you don't look in the phone book for a friend's number. You know it. This is your long-term memory. Your long-term memory has everything that you remember.

Why do you forget something? You did not learn it in the beginning. This is the major reason for forgetting. For example, you meet some new people, and you forget their names. You hear the names, but you do not learn them. Then you forget them.

1. Your short-term memory helps you _____
   (A) memorize new words you find in your reading materials.
   (B) remember a phone number for a little while.
   (C) spell English words correctly.
   (D) prepare for a test.

2. Your long-term memory enables you to _____
    (A) remember everything you come across every day.
    (B) remember things for no more than 30 seconds.
    (C) remember things every day and forget most of them.
    (D) remember your friend's phone number for a long time.

3. We tend to forget the names of the new people we have just met because _____
    (A) we did not try to memorize their names.
    (B) we did not hear their names clearly.
    (C) we have poor memories.
    (D) we didn't have time to memorize their names.

4. What is long-term memory?
    (A) Everything you learn.
    (B) All the names and phone numbers you know.
    (C) Things that take you a long time to remember.
    (D) Anything that you remember.

5. According to the author, how long does short-term memory last?
    (A) Until the next quiz.
    (B) Until you really learn something.
    (C) Less than half a minute.
    (D) As long as it takes to dial a phone number.

TEST 41 詳解

"Memorize these words." "Learn this spelling rule." "Don't forget the quiz tomorrow." You remember things *every day,* **but** how do you do it?

「把這些字背下來。」「學這個拼字規則。」「別忘了明天的小考。」你每天都在記事情，但你是如何辦到的？

memorize (ˈmɛməˌraɪz) *v.* 記憶；背誦　　**quiz** (kwɪz) *n.* 小考

You find a telephone number *in the phone book,* dial it, **and** **then** forget it. This is your short-term memory. It lasts *less than 30 seconds.* *However,* you don't look *in the phone book* for a friend's number. You know it. This is your long-term memory. Your long-term memory has everything ***that you remember.***

你在電話簿裡找到一個電話號碼，撥了它，然後就忘了這個號碼，這是你的短期記憶，只持續不到三十秒。然而，你不必查電話簿，就知道一位朋友的電話號碼，這是你的長期記憶。你所記得的每一件事，都屬於你的長期記憶。

dial (ˈdaɪəl) *v.* 撥（號）　　**short-term** (ˈʃɔrtˈtɝm) *adj.* 短期的
last (læst) *v.* 持續　　**long-term** (ˈlɔŋˈtɝm) *adj.* 長期的

Why do you forget something? You did not learn it *in the beginning.* This is the major reason *for forgetting.* *For example,* you meet some new people, **and** you forget their names. You hear the names, **but** you do not learn them. *Then* you forget them.

　　你爲什麼會忘記某件事情呢？因爲你在一開始就沒有去記。這就是會忘記的主要原因。例如，你剛認識一些新朋友，但很快就忘了他們的名字。你聽到他們的名字時，並沒有記下來，那麼你很快會就忘記。

major〔'medʒɚ〕*adj.* 主要的

1.(**B**) 你的短期記憶幫助你
　　(A) 記住閱讀時所發現的新字。　　(B) <u>暫時記得一個電話號碼。</u>
　　(C) 正確地拼出英文字。　　(D) 準備考試。
　　* *for a little while* 暫時

2.(**D**) 你的長期記憶使你
　　(A) 能記住每天所遇到的每件事。
　　(B) 只能維持記憶不過三十秒鐘。
　　(C) 每天記住一些事，而忘記大部分。
　　(D) <u>可以長久記得朋友的電話號碼。</u>
　　* *come across* 偶然遇見　　*no more than* 不超過；只有

3.(**A**) 我們很容易忘記剛認識的人的名字，因爲
　　(A) <u>我們並沒有努力去記他們的名字。</u>
　　(B) 我們沒有聽清楚他們的名字。
　　(C) 我們的記性很差。　　(D) 我們沒有時間記他們的名字。
　　* *tend to-V* 易於～

4.(**D**) 何謂長期記憶？
　　(A) 你所學過的每件事情。
　　(B) 你所知道的每個人名與電話號碼。
　　(C) 你需要花很久的時間才記得住的事情。
　　(D) <u>你所記得的一切事情。</u>

5.(**C**) 根據作者的說法，短期記憶會持續多久？
　　(A) 直到下一場小考。　　(B) 直到真的學會某事時。
　　(C) <u>不到半分鐘。</u>　　(D) 和撥一通電話的時間一樣久。

TEST 42

Read the following passage, and choose the best answer for each question.

Elephants are the largest land mammals in the world. They live on two continents, Africa and southern Asia. Asian elephants, also known as Indian elephants, are easier to tame than African elephants and have been domesticated for 4000 years. The elephants you see in the circuses and zoos are nearly always Asian. African elephants are larger and have great ears like fans. Both the African and Indian elephants have strong, tough skin and long, lovely tusks. That is their problem. Elephants are in danger. People kill these animals in order to use their skin and their tusks. Because of the massive killings, elephants are dwindling in number and it is feared that by the end of the century, these huge mammals may be extinct. However, elephants are problems in some parts of Africa. In areas where the largest herds exist, they have become giant pests to the farmers. No fence is strong enough to keep these monsters away from the crops. Elephants go where they wish, destroying food crops and farm buildings. African farmers wonder if they can allow the elephants to continue to exist in their neighborhood.

1. In a zoo, one will most likely see an Asian elephant because _____
   (A) Asian elephants can survive in a human environment.
   (B) Asian elephants are smarter than African elephants.
   (C) Asian elephants are easier to train than African elephants.
   (D) Asian elephants are more destructive than African elephants.

2. Based on the passage, elephants are killed because _____
   (A) they are pests to farmers.
   (B) they destroyed food crops and buildings.
   (C) they compete with humans for food and water.
   (D) their tusks and skin are valuable.

3. Which of the following statements is NOT true?
   (A) Elephants are the largest mammals in the world.
   (B) African elephants are larger than Asian elephants.
   (C) African elephants have created some problems for humans.
   (D) Elephants live on two continents, Africa and southern Asia.

4. The reason why elephants may become extinct by the end of the century is _____
   (A) that they have been domesticated by human beings.
   (B) that they are hunted by human beings.
   (C) that they are multiplying too fast.
   (D) that they are major pests to farmers.

5. Which of the following is NOT true of Asian elephants?
   (A) They are in danger.
   (B) They are not as large as African elephants.
   (C) They are killed for their valuable tusks.
   (D) Their skin is not as tough as that of African elephants.

TEST 42 詳解

Elephants are the largest land mammals *in the world*. They
live *on two continents, Africa and southern Asia.* Asian elephants,
also known as Indian elephants, are easier to tame *than African*
elephants **and** have been domesticated *for 4000 years.*

象是全世界上最大的陸上哺乳類動物，分佈在非洲與南亞兩大陸地。亞洲
象又名印度象，比非洲象容易馴服，被馴養已有四千年的歷史。

> mammal (ˈmæml̩) *n.* 哺乳類動物
> continent (ˈkɑntənənt) *n.* 大陸；洲
> tame (tem) *v.* 馴服   domesticate (dəˈmɛstəˌket) *v.* 馴養

The elephants *you see in the circuses and zoos* are *nearly always*
Asian. African elephants are larger **and** have great ears *like fans.*
在馬戲團與動物園裏看到的象，幾乎都是亞洲象。非洲象的體型較大，有像扇
子般的大耳朵。

> circus (ˈsɜkəs) *n.* 馬戲團   fan (fæn) *n.* 扇子

Both the African and Indian elephants have strong, tough skin
and long, lovely tusks. That is their problem. Elephants are in
danger. People kill these animals *in order to use their skin and*
their tusks.

非洲象和印度象都有堅韌的外皮，以及可愛的長牙。然而，這也是牠們的麻煩所在。大象正遭遇危險。人類爲了利用其表皮與長牙，而屠殺牠們。

tough〔tʌf〕*adj.* 堅韌的　　tusk〔tʌsk〕*n.* 象牙

Because of the massive killings, elephants are dwindling *in number*

and it is feared *that by the end of the century,* these huge mammals

may be extinct.

由於大量屠殺，象的數量正在減少中。到本世紀末，恐怕這些大型哺乳類動物可能會絕種。

massive〔'mæsɪv〕*adj.* 大量的　　dwindle〔'dwɪndl̩〕*v.* 減少
century〔'sɛntʃərɪ〕*n.* 世紀　　huge〔hjudʒ〕*adj.* 巨大的
extinct〔ɪk'stɪŋkt〕*adj.* 絕種的

However, elephants are problems *in some parts of Africa. In areas*

where the largest herds exist, they have become giant pests *to the*

farmers. No fence is strong *enough* to keep these monsters *away*

from the crops.

然而，大象在非洲某些地區也帶來問題。在大象群集的地區，牠們成了農夫眼中有害的大型動物。沒有堅固的圍籬，可使大象遠離農作物。

herd〔hɜd〕*n.* 群　　exist〔ɪg'zɪst〕*v.* 存在
giant〔'dʒaɪənt〕*adj.* 巨大的
pest〔pɛst〕*n.* 有害的生物；害蟲
fence〔fɛns〕*n.* 圍籬　　monster〔'mɑnstɚ〕*n.* 怪物

Elephants go *where they wish*, destroying *food crops and farm*

buildings. African farmers wonder *if they can allow the elephants*

to continue to exist in their neighborhood.

大象來去自如，破壞農作物與農舍。非洲的農夫正考慮，是否該讓大象繼續生存在他們的鄰近地區。

> crop〔krɑp〕n. 農作物　　wonder〔'wʌndɚ〕v. 想知道
> neighborhood〔'nebɚ͵hʊd〕n. 鄰近地區

1. (**C**) 動物園裏所見到的，可能大多是亞洲象，因爲

(A) 亞洲象能在人類的環境中生存。

(B) 亞洲象比非洲象聰明。

(C) <u>亞洲象比非洲象容易訓練。</u>

(D) 亞洲象比非洲象更具破壞性。

> * survive〔sɚ'vaɪv〕v. 存活　　smart〔smɑrt〕adj. 聰明的
> destructive〔dɪ'strʌktɪv〕adj. 有破壞性的

2. (**D**) 根據本文，大象被殺害是因爲

(A) 對農夫而言，牠們是有害的動物。

(B) 牠們破壞農作物和房舍。

(C) 牠們與人類爭食物和水。

(D) <u>牠們的長牙和皮很值錢。</u>

> * compete〔kəm'pit〕v. 競爭　　valuable〔'væljʊəbḷ〕adj. 有價值的

3. (**A**) 下列敘述何者爲非？

(A) <u>象是全世界最大的哺乳類動物。</u>

(B) 非洲象比亞洲象大。

(C) 非洲象爲人類製造了一些問題。

(D) 大象分佈在非洲與南亞兩大陸地。

4.(**B**) 大象可能在本世紀末絕種，因爲

    (A) 牠們已被人類馴服。

    (B) <u>牠們遭到人類獵殺。</u>

    (C) 牠們繁殖得太快。

    (D) 對農夫而言，牠們是主要的有害動物。

    * multiply〔'mʌltə͵plaɪ〕v. 繁殖

5.(**D**) 下列有關亞洲象的敘述，何者爲非？

    (A) 牠們正面臨危險。

    (B) 牠們不像非洲象那麼大。

    (C) 牠們因爲珍貴的象牙而被殺害。

    (D) <u>牠們的外皮不像非洲象那麼堅韌。</u>

> 利用早上吃早餐的時間看一篇，等公車無聊的時候看一篇，不要浪費時間查字典，快速做完本書，單字、片語，閱讀能力都能增加。

TEST 43

Read the following passage, and choose the best answer for each question.

Last spring my wife suggested that I call in a man to look at our lawnmower. It had broken down the previous summer, and though I promised to repair it, I had never got round to it. I would not hear of the suggestion and said that I would fix it myself. One Saturday afternoon, I hauled the machine into the garden and had a close look at it. As far as I could see, it only needed a minor adjustment: a turn of a screw here, a little tightening up there, a drop of oil and it would be as good as new. Inevitably, the repair job was not quite so simple. The mower firmly refused to mow, so I decided to dismantle it. The garden was soon littered with chunks of metal which had once made up a lawnmower. But I was extremely pleased with myself. I had traced the cause of the trouble. One of the links in the chain that drives the wheels had snapped. After buying a new chain I was faced with the insurmountable task of putting the confusing jigsaw puzzle together again. I was not surprised to find that the machine still refuse to work after I had reassembled it, for the simple reason that I was left with several curiously shaped bits of metal which did not seem to fit anywhere. I gave up in despair.

1. When the lawnmower broke down last summer, the writer _____
   - (A) immediately attempted to fix it.
   - (B) agreed to call in a repairman to take a look at it.
   - (C) promised to repair it himself.
   - (D) refused to have anything to do with it.

2. After a preliminary inspection of the mower, the writer concluded that _____
   - (A) the machine needed a complete overhaul.
   - (B) there was nothing seriously wrong.
   - (C) the job needed professional attention.
   - (D) it would be foolish for him to try the repair work.

3. The writer started to take the lawnmower apart _____
   - (A) the moment he laid his hands on the machine.
   - (B) because he was prompted by encouragement from his wife.
   - (C) for he deemed it impossible to spot the trouble without being told where it was.
   - (D) only after he had failed at his first attempt.

4. The cause which brought about all this trouble was finally discovered to be _____
   - (A) some missing screws.
   - (B) a few curiously shaped pieces of metal.
   - (C) want of lubricant.
   - (D) a broken piece in the driving chain.

5. To the writer, the whole experience was one of _____
   - (A) exasperation.
   - (B) exhilaration.
   - (C) accomplishment.
   - (D) exultation.

TEST 43 詳解

Last spring my wife suggested *that* I call in a man *to look at our lawnmower*. It had broken down *the previous summer*, *and though I promised to repair it*, I had *never* got round to it. I would not hear of the suggestion *and* said *that I would fix it myself.*

去年春天，我太太建議我，找個人來檢查我們的割草機。它在前年夏天就壞掉了，雖然我答應要修理，卻從沒找時間去做。我不聽從她的建議，並且說我會自己修理。

> lawnmower〔'lɔn,moɚ〕*n.* 割草機　　*break down* 故障
> *get round to* ~ 找時間去（做）~ 　　*hear of* 聽從

One Saturday afternoon, I hauled the machine *into the garden* **and** had a close look at it. *As far as I could see*, it *only* needed a minor adjustment: a turn *of a screw here*, a little tightening up there, a drop *of oil* **and** it would be *as good as* new.

有個星期六的下午，我把機器拖到花園，並且仔細地檢查了一下。就我所知，它只需要稍微調整一下：這裏的螺絲轉一轉，那裏再栓緊一點，再滴上潤滑油，它就會跟新的一樣了。

> haul〔hɔl〕*v.* 拖；拉　　minor〔'maɪnɚ〕*adj.* 較小的
> adjustment〔ə'dʒʌstmənt〕*n.* 調整　　screw〔skru〕*n.* 螺絲
> tighten〔'taɪtn̩〕*v.* 使變緊　　*as good as* 和~一樣

Inevitably, the repair job was not *quite so* simple. The mower

firmly refused to mow, *so* I decided to dismantle it. The garden

was *soon* littered with chunks of metal *which had once made up*

a lawnmower.

當然修理的工作並不簡單。割草機頑固地拒絕割草，因此我決定把它拆開來。
很快地，花園裡就散布著，一塊塊原先組裝成割草機的金屬零件。

> inevitably (ɪn'ɛvətəblɪ) *adv.* 必然地
> dismantle (dɪs'mæntḷ) *v.* 拆開　　litter ('lɪtɚ) *v.* 亂丟
> metal ('mɛtḷ) *n.* 金屬　　chunk (tʃʌŋk) *n.* 大塊；厚片

But I was *extremely* pleased with myself. I had traced the cause

of the trouble. One *of the links in the chain that drives the wheels*

had snapped. *After buying a new chain* I was faced with the

insurmountable task *of putting the confusing jigsaw puzzle together*

again. I was not surprised to find *that* the machine still *refuse to*

work *after I had reassembled it,* *for the simple reason that I was*

left with several curiously shaped bits of metal *which did not seem*

to fit anywhere. I gave up *in despair.*

但我卻沾沾自喜，因為我找出故障的原因了。轉動輪子的鍊條中，有一節斷了。買了新的鍊條後，我面臨到將那些令人困惑的拼圖，組合起來的困難差事。在我重新組合好之後，割草機仍不肯動。我並不驚訝，原因很簡單，我留下幾個什麼位置都不適合的奇怪的小金屬。我便絕望地放棄了。

> trace〔tres〕*v.* 查出；找到　link〔lɪŋk〕*n.*（鍊的）環
> chain〔tʃen〕*n.* 鍊　drive〔draɪv〕*v.* 驅動；推動
> snap〔snæp〕*v.* 折斷
> insurmountable〔͵ɪnsə'mauntəbḷ〕*adj.* 不能克服的
> *jigsaw puzzle* 拼圖　reassemble〔͵riə'sɛmbḷ〕*v.* 重新裝配
> curiously〔'kjurɪəslɪ〕*adv.* 奇特地
> shaped〔ʃept〕*adj.* 有特定形狀的　　*in despair* 絕望地

1. (**C**) 前年夏天，當作者的割草機故障時，作者
　(A) 馬上試著去修理它。　　　　(B) 同意找修理工人來檢查。
　(C) <u>答應要自己修理。</u>　　　　(D) 拒絕與它有任何關係。

　* attempt〔ə'tɛmpt〕*v.* 企圖　repairman〔rɪ'pɛrmən〕*n.* 修理工人
　have…to do with~ 與~有關

2. (**B**) 在初步的檢查過割草機之後，作者斷定
　(A) 機器需要一次徹底的大翻修。　(B) <u>沒有什麼大問題。</u>
　(C) 這需要專業的維修。　　　　(D) 試著去修理這機器是很愚蠢的。

　* preliminary〔prɪ'lɪmə͵nɛrɪ〕*adj.* 初步的
　inspection〔ɪn'spɛkʃən〕*n.* 檢查
　overhaul〔'ovə͵hɔl〕*n.* 檢修　attention〔ə'tɛnʃən〕*n.* 檢修

3. (**D**) 作者開始分解割草機，
　(A) 是在他一開始著手修理割草機的時候。
　(B) 因為他受到太太的鼓勵。
　(C) 他認為在沒有人告訴他問題在那裡的情況下，要把問題找出來是不可能的。
　(D) <u>是在他第一次嘗試修理失敗後。</u>

　* *take~apart* 分解~；拆開~　*lay one's hands on~* 著手（做）~
　deem〔dim〕*v.* 認為

4. (**D**) 結果發現，故障的主要原因是

　　(A) 一些遺失的螺絲釘。

　　(B) 一些形狀怪異的小金屬片。

　　(C) 缺少潤滑油。

　　(D) 驅動鍊條斷了一節。

　　* missing ('mɪsɪŋ) *adj.* 遺失的　　*want of~*　缺少~
　　lubricant ('lubrɪkənt) *n.* 潤滑油

5. (**A**) 對作者而言，這整個經驗是一件

　　(A) 惹人生氣的事。

　　(B) 令人興奮的事。

　　(C) 成就。

　　(D) 令人喜悅的事。

　　* exasperation (ɪg͵zæspə'reʃən) *n.* 激怒；生氣
　　exhilaration (ɪg͵zɪlə'reʃən) *n.* 令人興奮的事
　　accomplishment (ə'kɑmplɪʃmənt) *n.* 成就
　　exultation (͵ɛgzʌl'teʃən) *n.* 狂喜；喜悅

TEST 44

Read the following passage, and choose the best answer for each question.

It is a matter of common observation that although money incomes keep going up over the years, we never seem to become much better off. Prices are rising continuously. This condition is termed one of inflation; the money supply is becoming inflated so that each unit of it becomes less valuable. We have grown accustomed in recent years to higher and higher rates of inflation. What could be bought ten years ago for one dollar now costs well over two dollars. Present indications are that this rate of inflation is tending to rise rather than to fall. If in the real world, our money incomes go up at the same rate as prices, one might think that inflation does not matter. But it does. When money is losing its value, it lacks one of the qualities of a good money — stability of value. It is no longer acceptable as a store of value; and it becomes an unsuitable standard of deferred payments. Nobody wants to hold a wasting asset, so people try to get rid of money as quickly as possible. Inflation therefore stimulates consumer spending, and deters saving.

1. Over the years, our incomes have been increasing, and
   we _____
   (A) seem to prosper at a quicker rate.
   (B) are actually no better, if not worse, in our financial condition.
   (C) can afford to buy more of the things that we want.
   (D) have managed to keep prices down.

2. Inflation is a situation in which _____
   (A) we can watch our money increase in its value.
   (B) unemployment is no longer a problem.
   (C) people can always find better paying jobs.
   (D) money keeps losing its value.

3. If incomes and prices rise together, so the writer argues,
   (A) there will be no more market fluctuations.
   (B) money will hold its value.
   (C) inflation will remain to be a problem.
   (D) inflation poses no problem.

4. When money loses its value, _____
   (A) it is no longer stable.
   (B) its rate against gold will be kept at the same level.
   (C) goods will lose their value, thus creating no new problems.
   (D) incomes will keep stable to lessen the problems of inflation.

5. In a period of inflation, people are likely to _____
   (A) invest heavily on the stock market.
   (B) save money.
   (C) hold on to money as a dependable asset.
   (D) spend money and not bother to save.

TEST 44 詳解

It is a matter of common observation *that although* money incomes keep going up *over the years*, we never seem to become *much better off*. Prices are rising *continuously*. This condition is termed one *of inflation*; the money supply is becoming inflated *so that* each unit *of it* becomes less valuable.

一般人都察覺到，在過去幾年來，雖然我們金錢上的收入逐漸增加，但我們似乎沒有變得比較富裕，而物價卻一直不斷上漲。這種情況被稱爲是種通貨膨脹；貨幣的供給增加，因此每單位的幣值反而貶低了。

> common ('kɑmən) *adj.* 一般的
> observation (ˌɑbzɚ'veʃən) *n.* 觀察
> income ('ɪn,kʌm) *n.* 收入　　**better off** 情況良好；富裕
> term (tɝm) *v.* 稱爲　　inflation (ɪn'fleʃən) *n.* 通貨膨脹
> inflated (ɪn'fletɪd) *adj.* (通貨)膨脹的
> valuable ('væʃuəbl) *adj.* 有價值的

We have grown accustomed *in recent years* to higher and higher rates *of inflation*. What could be bought *ten years ago for one dollar now* costs well over two dollars. Present indications are *that* this rate *of inflation* is tending to rise rather than to fall.

近年來，我們逐漸習慣於愈來愈高的通貨膨脹率。十年前一塊錢可以買到的東西，現在值二塊錢以上。目前的跡象顯示，通貨膨脹率是傾向於上升，而非下降的。

> accustomed〔ə'kʌstəmd〕*adj.* 習慣的
> rate〔ret〕*n.* 比率　　***well over*** 遠超過
> present〔'prɛznt〕*adj.* 目前的
> indication〔,ɪndə'keʃən〕*n.* 指標；跡象
> ***tend to*** 傾向於　　***rather than*** 而不是

***If** in the real world, our money incomes go up at the same rate as prices*, one might think ***that** inflation does not matter. **But** it does.

假使在現實社會裡，我們的所得與物價等速率上升，大家可能會認為通貨膨脹是無關緊要的。事實上，它卻關係重大。

> rate〔ret〕*n.* 速率

When** money is losing its value*, it lacks one *of the qualities of a good money* — *stability of value*. It is *no longer* acceptable as a store *of value*; ***and it becomes an unsuitable standard *of deferred payments*.

當幣值貶低了，它就失去了良幣的其中一種特質 —— 幣值的穩定性。它不再被認為是具有保存的價值；而且它會變成延遲付款的一種不適當的標準。

> lack〔læk〕*v.* 缺乏　　stability〔stə'bɪlətɪ〕*n.* 穩定性
> store〔stor〕*n.* 儲存　　unsuitable〔ʌn'sjutəbḷ〕*adj.* 不適當的
> deferred〔dɪ'fɝd〕*adj.* 延緩的　　payment〔'pemənt〕*n.* 付款

Nobody wants to hold a wasting asset, *so* people try to get rid
of money *as quickly* **as possible**. Inflation *therefore* stimulates
consumer spending, **and** deters saving.

沒有人想要持有消耗性的資產，所以人們會儘快將錢花掉。因此，通貨膨脹會
刺激消費者消費，並妨礙儲蓄。

wasting (ˈwestɪŋ) *adj.* 消耗性的　　　asset (ˈæsɛt) *n.* 資產
stimulate (ˈstɪmjəˌlet) *v.* 刺激　　　defer (dɪˈfɝ) *v.* 妨礙；延緩

1. (**B**) 最近幾年，我們的收入不斷增加，但是我們
   (A) 似乎繁榮的速度更快。
   (B) 事實上財務狀況或許沒有變差，但並沒有變得更好。
   (C) 有能力購買更多我們想要的東西。
   (D) 設法維持低物價。

   * prosper (ˈprɑspɚ) *v.* 繁榮　　　manage (ˈmænɪdʒ) *v.* 設法

2. (**D**) 通貨膨脹的情況發生時，
   (A) 我們可以看到幣值增加了。
   (B) 失業就不再是問題。
   (C) 人們總是可以找到更高薪的工作。
   (D) 幣值持續貶低。

   * unemployment (ˌʌnɪmˈplɔɪmənt) *n.* 失業

3. (**C**) 正如作者所說，如果收入與物價同時上揚，
   (A) 將不再有市場波動的現象產生。
   (B) 幣值會持穩。
   (C) 通貨膨脹仍然會是個問題。
   (D) 通貨膨脹不會引起任何問題。

   * fluctuation (ˌflʌktʃuˈeʃən) *n.* 波動　　　pose (poz) *v.* 引起

4. (**A**) 當貨幣失去它的價值，

(A) 就不再穩定。

(B) 與黃金的比率會維持在相同的水準。

(C) 貨物也會失去它們的價值，因此不會有新的問題產生。

(D) 收入會維持穩定，以減少通貨膨脹的問題。

* stable〔'stebḷ〕*adj.* 穩定的　　lessen〔'lɛsṇ〕*v.* 減少

5. (**D**) 在通貨膨脹期間，人們可能會

(A) 大量投資於股市。

(B) 儲蓄。

(C) 守住金錢，認為錢是可靠的資產。

(D) 把錢花掉，不必費心儲蓄。

* stock〔stɑk〕*n.* 股票　　***hold on to*** 抓住
dependable〔dɪ'pɛndəbḷ〕*adj.* 可靠的
bother〔'bɑðɚ〕*v.* 費心；麻煩

團體訂購學生用書，有優待，可就近找各大
書局購買。

TEST 45

Read the following passage, and choose the best answer for each question.

COMMUTER BUS SERVICE
New York City — Brennan, N.J.
(Effective Sept. 1998 – May 1999)

SCHEDULE
- Buses leave Port Authority Bus Terminal, New York City, from 7:00 a.m., and every half-hour thereafter, until 11:30 p.m. (7 days a week)

- Buses leave Brennan station 20 minutes before and after every hour from 6:20 a.m. until 10:40 p.m. (7 days a week)

- Evening rush hours (5:00 p.m. to 7:00 p.m.) : buses leave Port Authority Terminal every 15 minutes (Monday-Friday)

- Holidays: buses leave every hour on the hour, each direction

  (Trip time: 30 minutes each way)

TICKETS
- One way: $ 1.50   • Commuter ticket (10 trips) : $ 10.00

- All tickets must be purchased at Window 12, Port Authority Bus Terminal, or at the Brennan station window BEFORE boarding buses.

---

1. At which of the following times does a bus leave New York for Brennan on Tuesdays?

   (A) 9:30 a.m.   (B) 11:15 a.m.

   (C) 2:45 p.m.   (D) 10:20 p.m.

2. If you had to meet a friend at the bus station in Brennan at 10:15 a.m. on a Friday, which is the latest bus you could take from New York?
   (A) The 10:00 a.m. bus.
   (B) The 9:30 a.m. bus.
   (C) The 9:00 a.m. bus.
   (D) The 8:20 a.m. bus.

3. What time does a bus leave Brennan for New York City on Saturdays?
   (A) 5:15 p.m.   (B) 7:10 p.m.
   (C) 9:40 p.m.   (D) 11:40 p.m.

4. Where should passengers buy their tickets?
   (A) From the driver before boarding the bus.
   (B) From the driver after boarding the bus.
   (C) At the door near this notice.
   (D) At a terminal ticket window.

5. If you need to take a bus on Christmas Day, what time will the bus leave?
   (A) 12:09 p.m.   (B) 12:45 p.m.
   (C) 12:30 p.m.   (D) 1:00 p.m.

TEST 45 詳解

通 車 服 務
紐約市 —— 紐澤西州布里蘭
（有效期間：自 1998 年 5 月至 1999 年）

時 刻 表

* 巴士自上午 7 時離開紐約市港務局站，而後每隔半小時一班，至晚上 11 點 30 分。（每週 7 天）

* 巴士每小時 20 分和 40 分各一班，自布里蘭車站開出。自上午 6 點 20 分至晚上 10 點 40 分。（每週 7 天）

* 晚上尖峰時間（下午 5 點至 7 點）：開離港務局站的巴士，每隔 15 分鐘一班。（自星期一至星期五）

* 例假日：各路線的巴士每小時正開出。

（旅程時間：每程 30 分鐘）

票 價

* 單程：1.50 元　　　　　* 定期票（10 程）：10 元

* 所有的車票必須上車「前」，在港務局站 12 號窗口，或布里蘭站的窗口購買。

---

commuter bus 固定往返兩地的公車
terminal〔ˈtɝmənḷ〕*n.*（巴士的）終點站；起站
thereafter〔ðɛrˈæftɚ, -ˈɑf-〕*adv.* 其後　　***rush hours*** 交通尖峰時間
on the hour 每小時正　　purchase〔ˈpɝtʃəs〕*v.* 購買
board〔bord〕*v.* 搭乘

---

1. (**A**) 星期二自紐約往布里蘭的巴士，是在下列哪一個時間開出？
   (A) 上午 9 點 30 分。　　　　(B) 上午 11 點 15 分。
   (C) 下午 2 點 45 分。　　　　(D) 下午 10 點 20 分。

2.(**B**) 如果在星期五上午 10 點 15 分，你必須和朋友在布里蘭車站見面，從紐約你能搭乘哪一班時間最近的巴士？
   (A) 上午 10 點的巴士。
   (B) 上午 9 點 30 分的巴士。
   (C) 上午 9 點的巴士。
   (D) 上午 8 點 20 分的巴士。

3.(**C**) 星期六什麼時間會有自布里蘭開往紐約的巴士？
   (A) 下午 5 點 15 分。
   (B) 晚上 7 點 10 分。
   (C) 晚上 9 點 40 分。
   (D) 晚上 11 點 40 分。

4.(**D**) 乘客應該在哪裡購買車票？
   (A) 上車前向司機購買。
   (B) 下車後向司機購買。
   (C) 在公告旁的門口購買。
   (D) 在巴士站的窗口購買。

5.(**D**) 如果你必須聖誕節當天搭巴士，巴士會在下列哪個時間開？
   (A) 下午 12 點 9 分。
   (B) 下午 12 點 45 分。
   (C) 下午 12 點 30 分。
   (D) 下午 1 點。

TEST 46

Read the following passage, and choose the best answer for each question.

The first bridges were pieces of wood that someone placed across a stream. These bridges were not very strong. If too many people tried to cross at one time the bridges broke. The people fell into the water! Later people made bridges of stone. The Romans made some very good bridges of stone and many of these are still standing today. Sometimes, however, no one could build a bridge across a river. The river was too wide and too deep and the water was too strong. If there was no bridge, the people had to use boats to cross it.

About two hundred years ago, a man named Darby built the first iron bridge. It crossed the River Severn in England. It was very strong and cars and trucks use it today. Bridge builders then began to use iron and steel to make two kinds of bridges. The first kind is the suspension bridge. "Suspension" means "hanging." There are usually two or more towers which hold up very strong cables. The ends of the cables are fastened at each side of the river. The bridge hangs down from the cables. The longest and most famous suspension bridge is the Golden Gate Bridge in San Francisco in the U.S. The other kind of steel bridge does not have cables. It is made in a number of different parts. Each ready-made part is very strong and joins on to the next part. One example of this kind of bridge is the Kuan-tu Bridge across the Tam-sui River in the northern part of Taiwan.

1. The least durable bridges are made of _____
   - (A) wood.
   - (B) stone.
   - (C) iron.
   - (D) steel.

2. The Romans were very successful in building _____
   - (A) wooden bridges.
   - (B) stone bridges.
   - (C) iron bridges.
   - (D) steel bridges.

3. The first iron bridge built two hundred years ago _____
   - (A) has fallen apart.
   - (B) can still be seen in the United States.
   - (C) crosses the river Thames.
   - (D) can still be used by automobiles today.

4. The Kuan-tu Bridge of Taiwan _____
   - (A) was built in the same way as the Golden Gate Bridge.
   - (B) used a lot of cables.
   - (C) was constructed by joining the parts together.
   - (D) is the longest bridge of its kind.

5. The Golden Gate Bridge in San Francisco is famous for its _____
   - (A) towers.
   - (B) length and structure.
   - (C) scenic views.
   - (D) iron and steel.

TEST 46 詳解

The first bridges were pieces of wood *that someone placed across a stream*. These bridges were not *very* strong. *If too many people tried to cross at one time* the bridges broke. The people fell into the water!

最早期的橋，是有人把幾塊木頭橫放在溪流上。這些橋不太堅固。如果同時有太多人想要過橋，橋就會斷裂，過橋的人就會掉到水裡！

place (ples) *v.* 放　　stream (strim) *n.* 小溪
cross (krɔs) *v.* 橫越

Later people made bridges *of stone*. The Romans made some *very* good bridges *of stone and* many *of these* are *still* standing *today*. *Sometimes, however*, no one could build a bridge *across a river*. The river was *too* wide and *too* deep *and* the water was *too* strong. *If there was no bridge*, the people had to use boats *to cross it*.

後來人們建造石橋。羅馬人建造了一些非常堅固的石橋，很多到現在仍然存在。然而，有時候人們無法在河上築橋，因為河太寬、太深，而且水流太強。如果沒有橋，人們就必須利用小船來渡河。

later ('letɚ) *adv.* 後來　　stand (stænd) *v.* 繼續存在
strong (strɔŋ) *adj.* 強有力的

About two hundred years ago, a man *named Darby* built the

first iron bridge. It crossed the River Severn *in England*. It was

very strong *and* cars and trucks use it *today*. Bridge builders *then*

began to use iron *and* steel *to make two kinds of bridges*.

大約兩百年前，一位名叫達比的人，建造了第一座鐵橋，橫跨英國的塞馮河。這座橋非常堅固，目前汽車和卡車都使用這座橋。然後建橋的人開始使用鐵和鋼來建築兩種橋。

iron (ˈaɪə·n) *n.* 鐵　　steel (stil) *n.* 鋼

The first kind is the suspension bridge. "Suspension" means

"hanging." There are *usually* two *or* more towers *which hold up*

very strong cables. The ends *of the cables* are fastened *at each*

side of the river. The bridge hangs down *from the cables*. The

longest and *most* famous suspension bridge is the Golden Gate

Bridge *in San Francisco in the U.S.*

第一種是吊橋。suspension 的意思是「懸吊」。通常有兩種或兩種以上的塔狀物，支撐著堅固耐用的纜索，纜索的末端固定在河的兩岸，橋就從纜索懸吊而下。最長且最聞名的吊橋，是美國舊金山的金門大橋。

suspension (səˈspɛnʃən) *n.* 懸吊　　***suspension bridge*** 吊橋
tower (ˈtaʊə·) *n.* 塔　　***hold up*** 支撐
cable (ˈkebḷ) *n.* 纜線；纜索　　end (ɛnd) *n.* 一端
fasten (ˈfæsṇ) *v.* 繫；綁

The other kind *of steel bridge* does not have cables. It is made

in a number of different parts. Each ready-made part is *very* strong

and joins on to the next part. One example *of this kind of bridge*

is the Kuan-tu Bridge *across the Tam-sui River in the northern*

part of Taiwan.

另外一種鋼橋沒有纜索，而是由許多不同的組件所形成。每一個做好的組件都很堅固，會和下一個組件連結起來。這種橋的一個實例，就是台灣北部橫跨淡水河的關渡大橋。

> *a number of* 很多的 (= *many*)；幾個 (= *several*)
> ready-made〔ˈrɛdɪˈmed〕*adj.* 做好的；現成的
> *join* (*on*) *to* 和～連結
> northern〔ˈnɔrðən〕*adj.* 北部的

1. (**A**) 最不耐用的橋是由 ＿＿＿＿＿＿＿ 所建造而成。
   (A) 木頭 (B) 石頭
   (C) 鐵 (D) 鋼
   * durable〔ˈdjʊrəbḷ〕*adj.* 耐用的

2. (**B**) 羅馬人非常成功地建造了
   (A) 木橋。 (B) 石橋。
   (C) 鐵橋。 (D) 鋼橋。

3. (**D**) 兩百年前建造的第一座鐵橋
   (A) 已經崩潰了。 (B) 在美國仍然可以見到。
   (C) 橫跨泰晤士河。 (D) 現在仍然可供汽車使用。
   * *fall apart* 崩潰   Thames〔temz〕*n.* 泰晤士河

4. (**C**) 台灣的關渡大橋

(A) 建造方式和金門大橋相同。

(B) 使用許多纜索。

(C) 是將各組件連結起來所建造而成的。

(D) 是同類的橋樑中最長的。

* construct ﹝ kən'strʌkt ﹞ *v.* 建造

5. (**B**) 舊金山的金門大橋，最有名的特色是在於它的

(A) 高塔。　　　　　　(B) 長度與結構。

(C) 美麗的景色。　　　(D) 鐵和鋼。

* scenic ﹝'sinɪk ﹞ *adj.* 風景優美的

看閱讀測驗查字典，會阻礙閱讀的速度，失去閱讀的興趣。單字不認識，用猜的，多看幾遍，實在不會，再查字典，此單字就不會忘記。

TEST 47

Read the following passage, and choose the best answer for each question.

If there is any single factor that makes for success in living it is the ability to profit by defeat. Every success I know has been achieved because the person was able to analyze defeat and actually profit by it in his next undertaking. Confuse defeat with failure, and you are indeed doomed to failure, for it isn't defeat that makes you fail; it is your own refusal to see in defeat the guide and encouragement to success.

Defeats are nothing to be ashamed of. They are routine incidents in the life of every man who achieves success. But defeat is a dead loss unless you do face it without humiliation, analyze it and learn why you failed. Defeat, in other words, can help to cure its own cause. Not only does defeat prepare us for success, but nothing can arouse in us such a compelling desire to succeed. If you let a baby grasp a rod and try to pull it away he will cling more and more tightly until his whole weight is suspended. It is this same reaction which should give you new and greater strength every time you are defeated. If you exploit the power which defeat gives, you can accomplish with it far more than you are capable of when all is serene.

1. What does the author know?
   (A) He knows at least several cases of success.
   (B) He knows every success in life.
   (C) He knows every success that has been achieved by man.
   (D) He knows every success that a particular person achieved.

2. Defeat is valuable _____
   (A) because it forces you to face it without humiliation.
   (B) in that it provides the guide and encouragement to success.
   (C) because of your own refusal to see in it the guide and encouragement to success.
   (D) since you refuse to see in it the guide and encouragement.

3. If you face defeat without humiliation, analyze it and learn why you failed, defeat _____
   (A) will become a dead loss.
   (B) is nothing but a dead loss.
   (C) is a dead loss according to the author.
   (D) is anything but a dead loss.

4. The baby will cling more and more tightly _____
   (A) as soon as you let him grasp a rod.
   (B) when you have pulled the rod away.
   (C) if you try to pull away the rod from his grasp.
   (D) unless you try to pull the rod away.

5. If you exploit the power which defeat gives, you can, according to the author, accomplish with it far more _____
   (A) than you have.
   (B) than the baby.
   (C) than your accomplishment.
   (D) than when there has been no defeat.

TEST 47 詳解

If there is any single factor **that** makes for success in living it

is the ability *to profit by defeat.* Every success *I know* has been

achieved **because** the person was able to analyze defeat **and** actu-

ally *profit by it in his next undertaking.*

人生中，如果有任何有助於成功的因素，那就是能自挫折中獲益的能力。
我所知道的每種成功，都是因爲當事人能分析挫折，並且能眞正從中獲益，進
而運用於下一次的任務中。

> single (ˈsɪŋg!) *adj.* 單一的　　factor (ˈfæktə) *n.* 因素
> **make for** 有助於　　profit (ˈprɑfɪt) *v.* 獲益
> **profit by** 從～中獲益 (= *profit from*)
> analyze (ˈæn!ˌaɪz) *v.* 分析　　defeat (dɪˈfit) *n.* 失敗；挫折
> undertaking (ˌʌndəˈtekɪŋ) *n.* 任務；事業

Confuse defeat with failure, **and** you are *indeed* doomed to failure,

for it isn't defeat **that** makes you fail; it is your own refusal to

see in defeat the guide and encouragement *to success.*

把失敗與挫折混爲一談，那你就眞的註定要失敗，因爲使你失敗的不是挫折，
而是你自己不肯從挫折中，去尋求成功的指引與鼓勵。

> **confuse…with～** 把…和～混淆　　**be doomed to** 註定
> refusal (rɪˈfjuz!) *n.* 拒絕　　guide (gaɪd) *n.* 指引
> encouragement (ɪnˈkɝɪdʒmənt) *n.* 鼓勵

Defeats are nothing *to be ashamed of.* They are routine incidents *in the life of every man **who** achieves success.* ***But*** defeat
is a dead loss *unless you do face it without humiliation, analyze it*
and learn why you failed.

挫折並不可恥，而只是每個成功的人，在人生中經常會有的事。但除非你
能不怕羞地面對挫折，去分析它，並且了解你為何失敗，否則挫折就變成不折
不扣的損失。

> ashamed (ə'ʃemd) *adj.* 感到羞恥的
> routine (ru'tin) *adj.* 例行的
> incident ('ɪnsədənt) *n.* 事件　achieve (ə'tʃiv) *v.* 達到
> humiliation (hju,mɪlɪ'eʃən) *n.* 丟臉；屈辱
> dead (dɛd) *adj.* 完全的

Defeat, *in other words,* can help to cure its own cause. ***Not only***
does defeat prepare us for success, ***but*** nothing can arouse *in us*
such a compelling desire *to succeed.*

換言之，挫折能幫助改正其本身的原因。挫折不僅能為我們的成功舖路，而且
也沒有其他的東西，能夠像挫折一樣，能激發我們，擁有如此強烈的追求成功
的渴望。

> *in other words* 換句話說　cure (kjʊr) *v.* 改正
> *prepare sb. for~* 為某人舖~路
> rouse (raʊz) *v.* 喚起；激勵
> compelling (kəm'pɛlɪŋ) *adj.* 強制性的；有強烈吸引力的

*If you let a baby grasp a rod **and** try to pull it away* he will cling more and more tightly **until** his whole weight is suspended. It is this same reaction **which** should give you new and greater strength **every time you are defeated.** *If you exploit the power **which** defeat gives,* you can accomplish **with** it far more **than** you are capable of **when all is serene.**

如果你讓嬰兒抓住一根棍子，而又試著把它拿走，嬰兒會愈握愈緊，直到他全身的重量都懸在棍子上爲止。每次當你受挫折時，也會有同樣的反應，會給你新的，而且更強的力量。倘若你利用這種挫折給你的力量，就可完成遠超過你未遭受挫折時所能完成的。

grasp〔græsp〕v. 緊抓　　rod〔rɑd〕n. 棍子
pull〔pʊl〕v. 拉　　cling〔klɪŋ〕v. 緊緊抓住
suspend〔sə'spɛnd〕v. 懸掛　　reaction〔rɪ'ækʃən〕n. 反應
exploit〔ɪk'splɔɪt〕v. 利用　　**be capable of** 能夠
serene〔sə'rin〕adj. 平靜的；寧靜的
all serene 一切正常；平安無事

1.（**A**）作者知道什麼？

(A) 他至少知道幾個成功的個案。
(B) 他知道人生中的每種成功。
(C) 他知道由人所達成的每種成功。
(D) 他知道某個特定的人的所有成功。

2. (**B**) 挫折是珍貴的，
  (A) 因爲它強迫你不怕羞地面對它。
  (B) <u>因爲它提供成功的指引與鼓勵。</u>
  (C) 因爲你自己不肯從挫折中，去尋找成功的指引與鼓勵。
  (D) 因爲你不肯從挫折中去尋找指標與鼓勵。
  * *in that* 因爲 (= *because*)

3. (**D**) 假如你能不怕羞地面對挫折，分析它，而且了解你爲何失敗，挫折
  (A) 會成爲全然的損失。
  (B) 只不過是全然的損失。
  (C) 依據作者的說法，是個全然的損失。
  (D) <u>絕對不是全然的損失。</u>
  * *anything but* 絕非

4. (**C**) 嬰兒會愈抓愈緊，
  (A) 一當你讓他抓住一根棍子。
  (B) 當你把棍子拿走。
  (C) <u>如果你想從他的手中把棍子拿走。</u>
  (D) 除非你想把棍子拿走。

5. (**D**) 依據作者的說法，假如你能利用挫折所給予的力量，就可完成遠超
  過 ＿＿＿＿＿＿ 所能完成的。
  (A) 你所擁有的事物　　　　　　(B) 嬰兒
  (C) 你的成就　　　　　　　　　(D) <u>你未遭受挫折時</u>

TEST 48

Read the following passage, and choose the best answer for each question.

"You'd better pick up a few things on the way."

"What do we need?"

"Some roast beef, for one thing. I bought a quarter of a pound coming from my aunt's."

"Why a quarter of a pound, Joan?" said Rogin, deeply annoyed. "That's just about enough for one good sandwich."

"So you have to stop at a delicatessen. I had no more money."

He was about to ask, "What happened to the thirty dollars I gave you on Wednesday?" but he knew that would not be right.

"I had to give Phyllis money for the cleaning woman," said Joan.

Phyllis, Joan's cousin, was a young divorcee, extremely wealthy. The two women shared an apartment.

"Roast beef," he said, "and what else?"

"Some shampoo, sweetheart. We've used up all the shampoo. And hurry, darling, I've missed you all day."

"And I've missed you," said Rogin, but to tell the truth he had been worrying most of the time. He had a younger brother whom he was putting through college. Joan had debts he was helping her to pay, for she wasn't working. She was looking for something suitable to do.

1. The conversation in the passage probably took place ⎯⎯⎯⎯
   (A) over the telephone.   (B) in Joan's apartment.
   (C) in Rogin's imagination.   (D) at a delicatessen.

2. One may go to a delicatessen ⎯⎯⎯⎯⎯
   (A) to buy some roast beef.   (B) to cash one's check.
   (C) to cool down.   (D) to buy some shampoo.

3. Joan explained to Rogin how she had spent the thirty dollars

   ⎯⎯⎯⎯⎯⎯

   (A) because Rogin insisted on knowing what had happened to it.
   (B) when Rogin said the amount wasn't right.
   (C) even though Rogin did not ask her to.
   (D) because she wanted Rogin to blame Phyllis.

4. Which of the following statements about Phyllis is true?
   (A) Though very rich, she cleaned the apartment to earn some
       extra money.
   (B) She shared an apartment with Joan's cousin.
   (C) She collected money from Joan, which she gave to the
       cleaning woman.
   (D) Her husband was probably away on some business.

5. Which of the following statements about Rogin is true?
   (A) He had been missing Joan all that day.
   (B) His greatest concern at this moment was money.
   (C) For financial reasons, he did not want his younger brother
       to get a college education.
   (D) He is an extremely selfish person.

TEST 48 詳解

"You'd better pick up a few things *on the way*."

"What do we need?"

"Some roast beef, *for one thing*. I bought a quarter of a pound *coming from my aunt's*."

「你最好在路上買些東西。」

「我們需要些什麼？」

「先買些烤牛肉。我從我姑媽家買了四分之一磅。」

* coming…aunt's 為分詞片語，修飾 pound。for one good sandwich 為副詞片語，修飾 enough。

> **pick up** 買　　**roast beef** 烤牛肉
> **for one thing** 首先

"Why a quarter of a pound, Joan?" said Rogin, *deeply annoyed*. "That's just about enough *for one good sandwich*."

"*So* you have to stop *at a delicatessen*. I had no more money."

「怎麼才四分之一磅，瓊？」羅金頗為生氣地說。「那大概只夠做個不錯的三明治。」

「所以你必須到熟食店去買。我沒有錢了。」

> delicatessen〔͵dɛləkə'tɛsn̩〕*n.* 熟食店

He was about to ask, "What happened to the thirty dollars *I gave you on Wednesday*?" *but* he knew *that would not be right*.

"I had to give Phyllis money *for the cleaning woman*," said Joan.

Phyllis, *Joan's cousin*, was a young divorcee, *extremely wealthy*. The two women shared an apartment.

他正想要問：「我星期三給你的三十元哪兒去了？」但他知道這樣問不太妥當。

「我必須給菲莉絲付清潔婦的錢。」瓊說。

瓊的堂姐菲莉絲，是個離了婚的年輕女人，非常富有。這兩個女人共住一間公寓。

* to ask 是不定詞，當 about 的受詞。I gave…Wednesday 是省略了 which 或 that 的形容詞子句，修飾 dollars。

> cousin〔ˈkʌzn̩〕*n.* 表（堂）兄弟姊妹
> divorcee〔dəˌvorˈsi〕*n.* 離了婚的人
> extremely〔ɪkˈstrimlɪ〕*adv.* 非常
> share〔ʃɛr〕*v.* 分享；共有

"Roast beef," he said, "*and* what else?"

"Some shampoo, sweetheart. We've used up all the shampoo. *And* hurry, darling, I've missed you *all day*."

「烤牛肉，」他說，「還要什麼？」

「一些洗髮精，親愛的。我們的洗髮精都用完了。要快點，親愛的，我一整天都很想你。」

> shampoo〔ʃæmˈpu〕*n.* 洗髮精

"And I've missed you," said Rogin, *but to tell the truth* he had been worrying *most of the time*. He had a younger brother *whom he was putting through college*. Joan had debts *he was helping*

her to pay, ***for she wasn't working.*** She was looking for something
suitable to do.

「我也想念妳，」羅金說。但是老實說，他大部分的時間都在煩惱。他要
供弟弟順利唸完大學。他還要幫瓊還債，因爲瓊現在沒工作，正在找合適的事
情做。

* whom…college 是形容詞子句，修飾 brother。he was…pay 是省略了
  which 的形容詞子句，修飾 debts。for 爲表原因的連接詞。suitable to
  do 爲形容詞片語，修飾 something。

> ***to tell the truth*** 老實說
> ***put through*** 順利完成　　debt〔dɛt〕*n.* 債務

1.(**A**) 本文中的對話可能是發生在

　(A) 電話中。　　　　　　　(B) 瓊的公寓裏。
　(C) 羅金的想像中。　　　　(D) 熟食店裏。

2.(**A**) 我們可以到熟食店裏

　(A) 買些烤牛肉。　　　　　(B) 將支票兌現。
　(C) 冷靜下來。　　　　　　(D) 買些洗髮精。

　* cash〔kæʃ〕*v.* 兌現

3.(**C**) 瓊向羅金解釋她如何花掉了那三十元，

　(A) 因爲羅金堅持要知道錢到哪兒去了。
　(B) 當羅金說那數目不對的時候。
　(C) 雖然羅金並沒問她。
　(D) 因爲她要羅金去責備菲莉絲。

　* ***insist on*** 堅持　　blame〔blem〕*v.* 責備

4.(**C**) 下列有關菲莉絲的敘述何者正確？

(A) 雖然她很有錢，但還是爲了賺些外快而清掃公寓。

(B) 她和瓊的堂姐同住一間公寓。

(C) 她向瓊收錢，再把錢付給清潔婦。

(D) 她丈夫大概因公出差去了。

* *on business* 因公事

5.(**B**) 下列有關羅金的敘述，何者正確？

(A) 他那天一直都在想念著瓊。

(B) 他目前最關心的是錢。

(C) 爲了財務方面的原因，他不想讓弟弟受大學教育。

(D) 他是個非常自私的人。

* concern〔kən'sɜn〕*n.* 關心的事
　 selfish〔'sɛlfɪʃ〕*adj.* 自私的

這本書如果讀不下去，就參加「劉毅英文模考班」，考試可以強迫你專心做閱讀測驗。

TEST 49

Read the following passage, and choose the best answer for each question.

One thing that startles visitors to London is the social status that animals enjoy there. Pet estimates indicate that there is at least one pet for every man, woman, and child in the city. Cats alone are estimated at five million. And to this figure must be added the dogs, birds, fish, ponies, rabbits, tortoises, monkeys, and other far more novel beasts which are privileged members of many a London household.

The most famous and favored of London's pets, however, do not share anyone's household. They have their own 34-acre estate in Regent's Park, the preserve of the Zoological Society of London since 1828. There are 7,000 of them, including the birds, beasts, and the 3,000 fish, and they are probably the most thoroughly observed, adored, and talked about animals alive. They are everyone's pets... or, at least, the pets of everyone who can squeeze in.

On a fine holiday afternoon 50,000 visitors may crowd into the London Zoo. In a year two million pay admission, about as many people as go to all of London's famous art galleries and museums. The feel of the place is evident on any sunny summer afternoon in the Children's Zoo, a special pets' corner. Here goats, ponies, donkeys, rabbits, lambs, parrots, pigeons, and even a reindeer and a baby elephant roam freely to kiss and to be kissed by tiny visitors. This special Children's Zoo was opened in 1935 to bring together zoo babies and London babies even more intimately than the larger enclosures would allow. Like many other Regent's Park "firsts," it has since been copied at zoos around the world.

1. Visitors to London are surprised that _____
   (A) the favorite household pet is a cat.
   (B) some Londoners keep rabbits and tortoises as household **pets.**
   (C) some Londoners keep squirrels as household pets.
   (D) animals enjoy social status.

2. There are as many pets in London as _____
   (A) there are houses.
   (B) there are inhabitants.
   (C) there are families.
   (D) there are privileged members.

3. "Tiny visitors" means _____
   (A) children.   (B) adults.
   (C) grown-ups.   (D) students.

4. The main idea in this selection is that _____
   (A) the London Zoo occupies a 34-acre estate in Regent's **Park.**
   (B) the inhabitants of London take great pride in their art **galleries** and museums.
   (C) Londoners are fond of household pets and of animals **in the zoo.**
   (D) London has a special zoo for children.

5. The best title for this selection is _____
   (A) London's Household Pets.
   (B) London's Famous Zoo.
   (C) London's Famous Art Galleries.
   (D) Zoo Babies and London Babies.

TEST 49 詳解

One thing *that startles visitors to London* is the social status *that* animals enjoy there. Pet estimates indicate *that* there is at least one pet *for every man, woman, and child in the city.* Cats alone are estimated at five million. *And to this figure* must be added the dogs, birds, fish, ponies, rabbits, tortoises, monkeys, *and* other *far more* novel beasts *which are privileged members of many a London household.*

會使到倫敦的遊客非常驚訝的是，在那裏的動物所享有的社會地位。關於寵物的統計數字顯示，在倫敦的每個男人、女人及小孩，至少都擁有一隻寵物。據估計，光是貓就多達五百萬隻。除了這個數目之外，還得加上狗、鳥、魚、小馬、兔子、烏龜、猴子，以及其他許多更稀奇古怪的動物，這些動物都是許多倫敦家庭的特權份子。

startle（'stɑrtḷ）v. 使吃驚　　pet（pɛt）n. 寵物

estimate（'ɛstəmɪt）v. 估計　n. 估計值

indicate（'ɪndə,ket）v. 指出　　figure（'fɪgjə）n. 數字

add（æd）v. 加上　　pony（'ponɪ）n. 小馬

tortoise（'tɔrtəs）n. 陸龜　　novel（'nɑvḷ）adj. 新奇的

beast（bist）n. 野獸；動物

privileged（'prɪvḷɪdʒd）adj. 有特權的

「many a ＋單數名詞」，表「許多的～」，相當於「many ＋複數名詞」。

household（'haʊs,hold）n. 家庭

The *most* famous and favored of London's pets, *however,* do not share anyone's household. They have their own 34-acre estate *in Regent's Park, the preserve of the Zoological Society of London since 1828.* There are 7,000 of them, *including the birds, beasts, and the 3,000 fish, and* they are *probably* the *most thoroughly* observed, adored, *and* talked about animals alive. They are everyone's pets... *or, at least,* the pets *of everyone who can squeeze in.*

　　但是在倫敦，最有名、而且最受喜愛的寵物，並不在任何人的家中，牠們在攝政公園裏，有自己的三十四英畝土地，也就是在一八二八年，所成立的倫敦動物學會的動物保護區。裏面的動物數目多達七千隻，包括各種鳥類、動物，以及三千條魚，牠們可能是最多人觀看、最被人喜愛，而且也是最常被人談論的活生生的動物。牠們是每個人的寵物…或者至少是，每個能擠入動物園的人的寵物。

　　favor〔'fevɚ〕v. 偏愛　　acre〔'ekɚ〕n. 英畝
　　estate〔ə'stet〕n. 地產；土地　　preserve〔prɪ'zɝv〕n. 禁獵區；保護區
　　zoological〔,zoə'lɑdʒɪkḷ〕adj. 動物學的　　society〔sə'saɪətɪ〕n. 學會
　　thoroughly〔'θɝolɪ〕adv. 徹底地　　alive〔ə'laɪv〕adj. 活的
　　adore〔ə'dor〕v. 喜愛　　squeeze〔skwiz〕v. 擠

On a fine holiday afternoon 50,000 visitors may crowd into the London Zoo. *In a year* two million pay admission, *about as many people as* go to all of London's famous art galleries and *museums.*

每逢晴朗的假日的下午，可能會有五萬名遊客，擠進倫敦動物園。每年有兩百萬個人，會付入場費，這就大約與每年參觀倫敦所有著名的美術館和博物館的總人數相等。

> ***crowd into*** 擠入　　admission〔ədˋmɪʃən〕*n.* 入場費
> gallery〔ˋgælərɪ〕*n.* 畫廊；美術館　　museum〔mjuˋzɪəm〕*n.* 博物館

The feel *of the place* is evident *on any sunny summer afternoon in the Children's Zoo, a special pets' corner. Here* goats, ponies, donkeys, rabbits, lambs, parrots, pigeons, ***and*** even a reindeer and a baby elephant roam *freely to kiss **and** to be kissed by tiny visitors.*

在兒童動物園這個特殊寵物的角落中，每逢晴朗的夏日午後，所給人的感受是強烈的。這裡有山羊、小馬、驢子、兔子、小羊、鸚鵡、鴿子，甚至有一頭馴鹿和一頭小象，自由自在地到處走動，去吻那些小遊客，或是被他們親吻。

> feel〔fil〕*n.* 感觸；感受　　evident〔ˋɛvədənt〕*adj.* 明顯的
> goat〔got〕*n.* 山羊　　donkey〔ˋdɑŋkɪ〕*n.* 驢子
> lamb〔læm〕*n.* 小羊　　pigeon〔ˋpɪdʒən〕*n.* 鴿子
> reindeer〔ˋrendɪr〕*n.* 馴鹿　　roam〔rom〕*v.* 漫步
> tiny〔ˋtaɪnɪ〕*adj.* 極小的

This special Children's Zoo was opened *in 1935 to bring together zoo babies and London babies even more intimately **than** the larger enclosures would allow. Like many other Regent's Park "firsts,"* it has since been copied *at zoos around the world.*

這座特別的兒童動物園，於一九三五年開幕，目的是要使幼小的動物，與倫敦的小孩，能更親密地聚在一起，而這是大範圍的動物園所辦不到的。就像其他許多**攝政**公園的「創舉」，兒童動物園自那時起，就被全球各地的動物園所模仿。

> intimately〔'ɪntəmɪtlɪ〕*adv.* 親密地
> enclosure〔ɪn'kloʒɚ〕*n.* 四周有圍牆的場地
> first〔fɝst〕*n.* 創舉　　copy〔'kɑpɪ〕*v.* 模仿

1. (**D**) 令倫敦的遊客吃驚的是
   (A) 大家最喜歡的家庭寵物是貓。
   (B) 有些倫敦人飼養兔子和烏龜當家庭寵物。
   (C) 有些倫敦人飼養松鼠當家庭寵物。
   (D) 動物享有社會地位。

   * squirrel〔'skwɝəl〕*n.* 松鼠

2. (**B**) 在倫敦，寵物的數目和 ＿＿＿＿＿＿ 一樣多。
   (A) 房子　　　(B) 居民　　　(C) 家庭　　　(D) 特權分子

3. (**A**) 「小遊客」是指
   (A) 小孩。　　(B) 成人。　　(C) 成人。　　(D) 學生。

   * grown-up〔'gron,ʌp〕*n.* 成人

4. (**C**) 本篇選文的主旨是
   (A) 在攝政公園中，倫敦動物園佔地三十四英畝。
   (B) 倫敦的居民非常以他們的美術館和博物館爲榮。
   (C) 倫敦人喜愛家庭寵物及動物園裏的動物。
   (D) 倫敦有座特殊的兒童動物園。

5. (**B**) 本篇選文最好的標題是
   (A) 倫敦的家庭寵物。　　　　(B) 倫敦著名的動物園。
   (C) 倫敦著名的美術館。　　　　(D) 幼小的動物與倫敦的小孩。

TEST 50

Refer to the following packaging label:

Servings per Package	4 —— one-cup size

Nutrition Information per Serving

Calories	120
Protein (grams)	1
Carbohydrate (grams)	25
Fat (grams)	1

Percentages of U.S. Recommended Daily Allowances (USRDA)

Protein	10
Vitamin A	4
Vitamin C	2
Thiamin	2
Riboflavin	15
Calcium	15
Niacin	**

** contains less than 2 % of USRDA

1. How many half-cup servings are there per package?
   - (A) 4
   - (B) 8
   - (C) 120
   - (D) 25

2. How many calories are there in two servings?
   - (A) 120
   - (B) 60
   - (C) 240
   - (D) 480

3. Which of the following nutrients is not found in appreciable amounts?

   (A) vitamin C
   (B) vitamin A
   (C) niacin
   (D) riboflavin

4. What do the letters RDA signify?

   (A) Registered with the Department of Agriculture.
   (B) Riboflavin, vitamin A and vitamin D.
   (C) Redistribution Amounts.
   (D) Recommended Daily Allowances.

5. If you want to regulate your calorie intake to about 2000 calories per day, how many packages could you eat in one day?

   (A) 1
   (B) 4
   (C) 15
   (D) 20

TEST 50 詳解

參考下列包裝的標籤：

每包的份量	4 份（每份為一杯之量）
每份之營養成份表	
卡路里	120
蛋白質（克）	1
碳水化合物（克）	25
脂肪（克）	1
美國政府推薦的每日攝取量的百分率（USRDA）	
蛋白質	10
維他命 A	4
維他命 C	2
維他命 B_1	2
維他命 B_2	15
鈣	15
菸鹼酸	**
** 含量低於 USRDA 的百分之二	

packaging〔'pækɪdʒɪŋ〕*n.* 包裝　　label〔'lebḷ〕*n.* 標籤

serving〔'sɝvɪŋ〕*n.* 一份；一客　　package〔'pækɪdʒ〕*n.* 小包；小袋

nutrition〔nju'trɪʃən〕*n.* 營養　　calorie〔'kælərɪ〕*n.* 卡路里

protein〔'protiɪn〕*n.* 蛋白質　　gram〔græm〕*n.* 公克

carbohydrate〔'kɑrbo'haɪdret〕*n.* 碳水化合物

fat〔fæt〕*n.* 脂肪　　percentage〔pə'sɛntɪdʒ〕*n.* 百分比

recommend〔ˌrɛkə'mɛnd〕*v.* 推薦

allowance〔ə'lauəns〕*n.* 定量；限額

vitamin〔'vaɪtəmɪn〕*n.* 維他命

thiamin〔'θaɪəmɪn〕*n.* 維他命 B_1（= *thiamine*）

riboflavin〔ˌraɪbə'flevɪn〕*n.* 維他命 B_2

calcium〔'kælsɪəm〕*n.* 鈣　　niacin〔'naɪəsṇ〕*n.* 菸鹼酸

1. (**B**) 每包有多少個半杯的份量？

    (A) 4 個　　　(B) <u>8 個</u>　　　(C) 120 個　　(D) 25 個

2. (**C**) 兩份有多少卡路里？

    (A) 120 卡　　(B) 60 卡　　　(C) <u>240 卡</u>　　(D) 480 卡

3. (**C**) 下列何種營養素的量是估計不出來的？

    (A) 維他命 C　　　　　　　　(B) 維他命 A

    (C) <u>菸鹼酸</u>　　　　　　　　　(D) 維他命 B_2

    * nutrient ('njutrɪənt,'nu-) *n.* 營養素

    appreciable (ə'priʃɪəbḷ) *adj.* 可察覺的；可估計的

4. (**D**) 字母 RDA 意指什麼？

    (A) 向農業部登記。

    (B) 維他命 B_2、維他命 A，和維他命 D。

    (C) 重新分配量。

    (D) <u>推薦的每日攝取量。</u>

    * signify ('sɪgnə,faɪ) *v.* 表示…之義

    Department of Agriculture 農業部　　register ('rɛdʒɪstɚ) *v.* 登記

    redistribution (,ridɪstrə'bjuʃən) *n.* 重新分配

5. (**B**) 如果你想控制每天的卡路里攝取量約為 2000 卡，那麼每天可以吃

    幾包？

    (A) 1 包　　　(B) <u>4 包</u>　　　(C) 15 包　　(D) 20 包

    * regulate ('rɛgjə,let) *v.* 控制　　intake ('ɪn,tek) *n.* 攝取量

    ※ 這條題目是算術題，參加「全國高中英文閱讀測驗大賽」的同學，很多都

    選答案 (C)。

心得筆記欄

中級英語閱讀測驗

售價：180 元

主　　　編 / 劉　毅

發　行　所 / 學習出版有限公司　　☎ (02) 2704-5525

郵 撥 帳 號 / 05127272 學習出版社帳戶

登　記　證 / 局版台業 *2179* 號

印　刷　所 / 裕強彩色印刷有限公司

台 北 門 市 / 台北市許昌街 10 號 2F　　☎ (02) 2331-4060

台灣總經銷 / 紅螞蟻圖書有限公司　　☎ (02) 2795-3656

本公司網址 / www.learnbook.com.tw

電 子 郵 件 / learnbook@learnbook.com.tw

2020 年 1 月 1 日新修訂

4713269383444